Upon the Eastern Sun

A novel of the Civil War

Jonathan Perkins

xulon PRESS

Copyright © 2012 by Jonathan Perkins

Upon The Eastern Sun
A Novel of the Civil war
by Jonathan Perkins

Printed in the United States of America

ISBN 9781624193774

All rights reserved solely by the author. The author guarantees all contents are original and do not infringe upon the legal rights of any other person or work. No part of this book may be reproduced in any form without the permission of the author. The views expressed in this book are not necessarily those of the publisher.

Unless otherwise indicated, Bible quotations are taken from the King James Version. Copyright © 1976 by Bible House, and the New International Version, copyright © 1988 by Tyndale Publishing.

www.xulonpress.com

To my wife Amanda, the reason I kept going.

Prologue

Ecclesiastes 3:8

*A time to love, and a time to hate;
a time of war, and a time of peace.*

May 2, 1863

The darkness of night and translucent thoughts plagued him...

A flash of light from the tree line blinded him, the pain rushing through his arm silenced his thoughts as he fell to the cold hard ground beneath his mount...

His arm fell limp off of the stretcher as the bearers stumbled to the ground...

"Pray gentlemen... pray," stated the doctor.

****

A slow constant patter of rain battered the windowpane in the room as the silence rang loudly out within the afternoon. The baby's soft cry broke the deafening sound of nothingness as his groggy eyes came awake part way before falling down to the bags beneath them. Each strained heartbeat brought upon a heavy breath, the chest rising quickly but descending deeply...

May 10, 1863

"Order A.P. Hill to prepare for action. Pass the infantry to the front! Tell Major Hawks...."

Gasping, the general weakly continued to speak. "Let us pass over the river and rest under the shade of the trees."

The general breathed heavily, his chest rising and falling, the sheets moving in the sun spattered rhythm. Then it stopped. Each person watched and held their breath waiting to see the chest rise again.

"He is dead."

****

A slow moving dirge was being played by a brass band marching in front of the funeral procession. The horse's hooves clomped, while the wheels of the hearse clacked along the cobblestone road. The coffin, draped with the Confederate flag, gently bounced in the glass covered wagon, while soldiers from Virginia marched behind it.

Hordes of people lined the street to the cemetery. Some standing for hours, legs tired and cramping wanting to catch a glimpse of the casket. They lined ten rows deep in various dress and orientation. From suits to rags, from men to women, from European to African, the tears flowing the same from the tear ducts down to the collar bone.

A mourning hush fell over the crowd, all eyes fixated upon one man. All that was heard was the crunching of gravel under boots and shoes, the occasional cry of a baby and the flags that gently danced their patriotic promenade in the breeze.

Prologue

Amidst the crowd stood the lonely woman of Virginia, the widow of the Confederacy. Her thick black veil that covered her young face and fresh tears was attached to a black bonnet covering her dark strands of hair that wanted to blow free in the wind. Her black dress flowed from her shoulders to her ankles, slightly rippling in the breeze of the day.

She clung to her handkerchief, tightly gripping the cloth. Anna Jackson watched as the band slowly marched while playing *Rock of Ages*. Slowly and deathlike, she turned her attention to the black horses, strapped down with leather harnesses, two legs moving in front of the other.

The hearse rolled in front of her, the sun glinting off its glass and wood coverings. She watched the casket slowly pass by, watched it take her husband and she waved with such finality that caused her to weep. The *Stonewall* to the Confederacy, *her* stone wall to lean on was gone.

In the distance, the Army of Northern Virginia was preparing to move. The wagons were filled, horses watered and rested. They began to move northward, moving out of Virginia. The 60,000 men marched their way, faithfully leading them to Pennsylvania.

Chapter One

1 Chronicles 12:8b

They were brave warriors, ready for battle and able to handle the shield and spear. Their faces were the faces of lions, and they were as swift as gazelles in the mountains.

Army of Northern Virginia

June 30, 1863

The crickets seemed to be in an argument with each other as they continued to phonate off louder than the next. They filled the early morning air with that distinctive chirp they reverberated during the heat of the summer. The heat and humidity had battered both sides of the war and the men felt as though Hell had come to Pennsylvania to wreak havoc on their invasion.

Sweat dripped off the man's body, soaking his wool blanket with the wetness. The stickiness of the humidity and the sound of the tweeting crickets caused his eyes to open. He stood to his bare feet and rubbed his toes in the grass; even that was warm. Sliding his suspenders over his shoulders, he stepped over to an unlit lamp hanging from a tree branch, the flame obviously had blown out during the night.

The eastern sky began to display colorful rays that peeked over the horizon.

Striking a match, he relit the lamp and stared for a moment at the flame behind the glass. He gazed as it danced, then he removed his gold pocket watch from his trouser pocket, the chain swinging from the force. Using the lamp to illuminate the face, he glanced at the time. Not yet five o'clock in the morning.

As he stood with his arms outstretched, attempting to expel the sleep from his aching body, an older sergeant approached.

"Lieutenant Joshua Anderson? I got a message from Captain Robinson," the sergeant stated in his deep Southern accent.

"Thank you, Sergeant Baxter," retorted Joshua as he received the note and read it.

> *Lieutenant Anderson,*
> *Col. Fry has instructed me, per General Archer, to send the company east along the Chambersburg Pike. Send out flankers from your platoon. Strike camp immediately.*
> *Captain Robinson*

Joshua turned the note over and scratched his initials onto it after saying he would comply. Returning the note to the heavily bearded Alabamian Sergeant, he said, "Take this to Captain Robinson with my compliments, Sergeant. Before you leave... have you heard from home lately?" he asked nervously.

"Not a lick sir. You?"

"Nah."

"Confederate mail don't move too quick. I best get back now sir," the stout middle aged sergeant replied as he turned and stalked his way back to his camp leaving Joshua alone

Chapter One

with the crickets and ever growing incandescence of the sun rising over the tree line.

Once the sergeant was out of sight, he looked to the dark sky above his head and felt a small mist tickle his whiskers. "Home."

****

The overcast clouds blocked out the sun's rays that beamed far above the ground, but even they could not stop the humid air from attacking. In fact, the clouds seemed to act as a blanket wrapped around the earth trapping in the humidity. They slowly darkened and a light mist began to descend to the earth. Tiny puddles began to form outside the tent of General Heth.

His brown hair was ruffled from the brief but arduous night's sleep. Stepping outside his tent, leaving his overcoat slung over a chair, he stretched out his suspenders and slid them over his shoulders. He looked to the sky, allowing the mist to dash his face with the awakening power of God. Blowing out a long hot breath, he began to pray softly to himself. *Oh heavenly Father, use me as you will. Give me your wisdom, Father. Give us the tools to strike down our enemies.*

Bringing his eyes down from the heavens, he opened them to notice Major Finney ambulating through the rows of tents. His face was bright and cheery, his flowing black mustache slightly blowing in the day's breeze. His sword bobbed from side to side with each step.

"How are you this morning, Major Finney?"

"I am fine, sir, and how are you?"

"I will be better once the day gets longer."

"You look a bit worn this morning General. Are you all right, sir?" the major asked, his brows scrunched and chin lifted in genuine concern.

"I am fine, Major, thank you. Just a bit tired. A day of riding will make me feel better."

"Yes, sir. Well sir, I have duties to perform, I will show myself to them."

Heth sat at his desk which was outside of his tent underneath a canopy. His chair sank a little in the dirt as his weight pushed into it. The papers in front of him were disheveled from the night breeze. Straightening them and putting them away made him see a paper that he was not sure he had seen before. He read it, but then looked around to see if anyone was near before reading it more carefully. His eyes became large and his brow pinched together.

****

Swaying from side to side in the saddle, the leather moaned from the weighted movement as Joshua wiped his forehead that was damp with sweat. Putting the rag back into his pocket, he returned his hand to the brown leather reins. The light rain falling did nothing to cool his forehead, only caused the dirt to cake up on the back of his neck. However, it did settle the dust of the road.

The chattering of the army was a fantastic conversation to the ears of the trees, lifting the noise deeply throughout the land. Amidst this great discord of sound came a rider galloping toward Joshua.

"Lieutenant Anderson, Colonel Fry wants you to ride to that hill right yonder," a corporal yelled, pointing two gloved fingers at the hill. "He wants ya to look ahead and report how we are moving."

"Very well Corporal. Wait here and I'll report back."

Joshua dug his heels into the ribs of his mount, squeezing her sides. Galloping toward the hill on the forward right of the army's formation, the horse moved with long elegant strides. Her mane flowed from the wind of her movement,

Chapter One

hooves pounding the hardened sod below. He bounced dutifully within the confines of the stirrups and saddle, slightly lifting his bottom up as he rode.

He pulled back on the reins after reaching the crest of the hills. The black and white mare slowed and halted at the top, snorting as she did. Joshua drew out his looking glass and viewed the plush green rolling hills abounding in front of him. Fields of corn and wheat gently swayed in the breeze. The sweat from his forehead dripped onto the golden colored metal of his looking glass.

"Where is Stuart?" Joshua stated aloud while patting his horse's neck. "He should be out in front, not General Pettigrew's men. What is he doing? Maybe he is searching for a new banjo?" he chuckled.

Joshua lifted the glass back to his eye and watched General Pettigrew's division heading toward Cashtown, while at the same time looking for any kind of movement along the flanks. The light rain falling from above spattered the glass, making it difficult to see.

Pulling back on the left rein, Joshua commanded his mare to turn around. Feeling the kick of her driver, she began to gallop back to the 13th Alabama Regiment and the rest of his platoon. Her movements were swift, muscles bulging as each leg and hoof basted the ground below causing clumps of dirt to be lifted through the air.

"Corporal," Joshua told the waiting man after reaching his platoon, "tell Colonel Fry that Pettigrew's men are moving just fine. No enemy to report."

"Yes, sir. The colonel sends his compliments."

The rider left Joshua with his men walking along the Chambersburg Pike. Their feet were sore, some bare, others sheathed with boots or cloth. The calloused skin of the bare footed men had broken open, dirt infecting their feet. He dismounted his horse and began to walk, turning around and looking at his men. He nodded his head at them and they continued on their way.

****

General Pettigrew lightly bit off the end of a long brown cigar, spitting out the loose end from his mouth. He ran his fingers through his brown, slightly graying bearded chin, whisking from it the loose tobacco strands. He stood from his chair and looked outside at the light just coming up from the dark sky. A small tint of blue and green began to form outside the opening emanating through his brain. He began to pace.

"General Pettigrew?"

"Hmm?"

"General Heth wants you, sir."

"Thank you Major. I'll be there."

Grudgingly, Pettigrew stopped pacing and returned his brain to the present day. His blue with gold trim suspenders hung from his body, swaying with the motion. Setting his cigar gently down, he pulled his suspenders over the long-sleeved discolored white shirt. He picked up his gray jacket holding the gold stars on the collar, from the edge of the bed and slung it over his broad shoulders.

General Johnston Pettigrew wrapped his leather belt around his waist, cinching to it the sword and scabbard. Straightening his shoulders, he smoothed out the wrinkles and creases in his tunic. Sighing heavily, and cursing the heat under his breath, he picked up his cigar and returned it to his mouth. Turning to the flap of his tent, he retrieved his kepi and stepped outside.

As he donned his headpiece, the smell of beef filled his nostrils with that familiar scent of meat cooking on skillets over an open flame. Pettigrew's stride took him down wooden planks that had been laid down in the mucky grass.

Chapter One

The black boots on his feet clopped and clogged on the shaky wooden path.

He did not walk far before reaching Heth's headquarters. Aides rushed about, papers and maps were shuffled, coffee steamed from within tin cups and orders were shouted to subordinate officers. Major Finney came swiftly to the General after announcing Pettigrew's presence to Heth.

"General Heth is waiting, sir. Do go in."

Upon entrance to the tent, Heth sat up from his chair.

"James."

"Sir."

"Good to see you well this morning. I have orders from General Hill to move out this morning and move past Cashtown. I will be putting your brigade out in front, leading the march."

Pettigrew smiled, "Very well sir."

"I want advance flankers and our scouts to be fully alert. Without Stuart it's hard to know what is out there. I see a town beyond Cashtown that looks as though water could be found and I also hear from reports that there is a shoe factory there. Perhaps we could find some for the men."

"Yes, sir."

****

Army of the Potomac

June 30, 1863

"Captain Spalding!"

"Hmm?"

"Sir, you awake?"

"What?" asked Spalding in a hoarse whisper.

"General Buford wants you."

"Oh" Spalding said, letting the message sink into his groggy brain still in a fog, "Oh! Thank you Corporal Bryant."

The captain swung his feet around and set them on the warm grass below his cot. His right hand combed through his ear length blond hair, while his left pinched the bridge of his nose with his forefinger and thumb. He sighed a heavy and slumber-some sigh.

Rising to his feet, he slid on his trousers, buttoning the pants tight. His bent knees creaked and ached from the day's ride, bowing slightly. Putting on his blue tunic over his shoulders, he stretched before fastening the brass buttons that were stamped with an eagle. He looked around, head turning about, attempting to locate his sword, while moving to his desk which was a catastrophe of strewn about maps and papers.

Captain James Spalding sifted through them before finding his sword and belt hidden underneath. Wrapping the black leather around his waist, he pulled it tight before turning his attention back to his maps. Neatly folding the latter, he tucked them into his saddle bag and threw it over his shoulder.

Moving to the flap of his tent, he was about to cast the flap open but stopped short. Turning around, he looked across his tent through the dim light of the slightly flickering lamp at the picture of his beloved wife on his desk. His brows scrunched together and his eyes narrowed. The lines on his forehead bore deep into his skull as his mustache tickled his pursed lips. Closing his eyes for a moment, Jim whispered a prayer before exiting the tent.

As he walked, outside the sun was seemingly still deep in its slumber, the only lights to be seen were the glowing embers of burned out campfires, lamps hanging and fireflies dancing in the breeze. The humidity that scorched the air caused heat lightning to fill the clouded sky above his head. He put on his wide brimmed riding hat and walked down a

Chapter One

pathway leading to a faded red barn, its white trim chipped and peeling. The structure was surrounded by a weathered fence with missing pickets here and there.

James entered at the front of the barn via the small hill leading up to the large hinged doors. "Captain Spalding reporting as ordered, sir."

"Enter."

He moved past empty stalls that once contained livestock. The odor of hay and excrement was slight, but still obvious enough to make him scrunch his nose at first inhalation. General Buford stood staring out a window from within an abandoned stall, arms behind his back, fingers interlocked.

"Still dark as night, yet hot as hell out there," said the General. "Jim, put your maps on the table."

Buford turned slightly and pointed at a small barn door propped up on hay stacks. The General lit his pipe, the sulfuric smell permeated the air until it was strangled out by the sweet smell of tobacco.

James began to spread out the parchment paper maps on the makeshift table, while General Buford turned around. "I need to see Pennsylvania. We'll be leaving the Fairfield area early."

"Yes, sir," replied James unfolding a different map.

"Jim, we are riding ahead of the main body today. We are going to try and catch up with those rebs who stampeded Fairfield. We could have gotten 'em last night, but…they sure did scare the townsfolk. Regardless, I want to scout out the Rebel force and see where all the players are."

"Well, sir. We uh…well, we should ride northwest. Our last intelligence puts the rebs heading toward Harrisburg. Looking at the topographical map, that could prove disastrous. They would be well entrenched with good ground before we could concentrate any legitimate force."

"Well…I would like to be at…" Buford trailed off for a bit as he scanned the map, "Emmitsburg and then move out

Upon The Eastern Sun

from there on the Emmitsburg Road to head north. I hear cavalry is up there; Kilpatrick's boys. Maybe link up with them, see what they know."

"Yes, sir."

"Well, get your boys moving. We have a long day ahead of us."

"Yes, sir,"

Buford returned to the maps one more time. "I'd like to get to this town here," he pointed "where all the roads meet. That's where I hear General Kilpatrick's boys are. Right here." Buford said tapping his finger.

"Gettysburg, sir?"

****

"Sir, it's time to get up. The men need their orders, sir."
"Mmm?"

"Sir, I know you're tired. We're all tired."

"I know. I know." The gruff man came to a sitting position in his cot, the upper half of his body still teetering from exhaustion. He sighed heavily before attempting to speak. "Ugh." Reaching for a canteen, his aide handed him a tin cup filled with water. The cool liquid slithered into his stomach to revive him. "Thank you!"

"I'm sorry sir. The other generals are restless. They want their orders, General Meade."

"Ok. Ok. Can you believe, this time two days ago I was just a corp commander? They woke me up, sort of like you did" Meade snickered. "Thought I was being arrested."

"Yes, sir."

"They tell me I am 'in command of the Army of the Potomac'. Straight from President Lincoln himself. Hard to believe."

The aide stood silent, watching General Meade put on his trousers, then button the upper half of his shirt, while all the

Chapter One

time holding the General's tunic in his hands. Meade shoved his boot over the top of his foot and stomped the ground before standing and letting the aide put his coat overtop his shoulders.

Meade wiped the sleep from his eyes and brushed his dark hair back behind his ears while straightening his beard. "Well…ready. Please rustle me up some breakfast and coffee."

"Yes, sir" the aide said as he rushed from the tent leaving Meade looking in his mirror.

"Two days ago…".

****

James put his left foot into the stirrup, his hand grasping the mane of the mount. Pushing off of his right leg, he swung it around the hind haunches and pulled himself upon the gelding. Digging his heel into the ribs of the horse, he moved up next to Lieutenant Colonel William Markell, the 8th New York's Regimental Commander.

"Are the men in formation again?" asked Markell.

"Sir?"

"Oh, it's you Jim."

"May I join you for the ride today?"

"Permitted. You want to ride with Matt?"

"If you don't mind sir. I want to talk to my brother-in-law, but he is with your regiment."

"Not a problem."

He rode with the colonel for a short while, the two men not really speaking. James allowed the silence to carry his mind back home. Home to rivers and trees winding around each other, never knowing where one started and the other ended. As the scent of pine trees entered his nostrils, James closed his eyes and thought of his wife. He re-entered reality when the colonel cleared his throat.

"Sir, why didn't we attack the enemy at Fairfield?" asked James.

"It is off our route to Emmitsburg. General Buford did not want to do anything against plans."

They continued to ride, again neither speaking much, while a light rain fell upon their necks. The sounds of horses' clicking hooves on the dirt road beneath them rose to their ears. The constant chatter of men, the equipment jingling as they rode, leather moaning and creaking were sounds to their ears. The presence of the looming war was a deafening noise that resounded in their minds.

Breaking the silence was Colonel Markell, "How is that young bride of yours?"

"The last I heard she was still back in Rochester about to have the baby. Of course that was three weeks ago, sir."

"Well, mail moves a little slow."

"Yes, sir."

"Do not worry though. Women have been having children for many, many years…without the help of men, I might add. I am sure she is doing just fine."

"Yes, sir. Thank you."

"Spalding, you can ride with Matt. No need to keep riding with me.

"Yes, sir."

James pulled to the right on his reins, moving toward the rear of the column to get to Matt's company. Most of the faces were familiar, some from Rochester, New York, his home, his city. Others were from the surrounding area of the finger-shaped lakes.

He reached the area where Matt was riding. "Where to Captain?" Matt called out.

"Pennsylvania," smirked James knowing Matt already knew, "Gettysburg."

****

Chapter One

He sat in his rocking chair, hands folded in his lap, creaking back and forth on the wooden floor. Through the window slats he could see the light slowly creeping its way up over the humid horizon, sullen clouds looming in the air. His pant legs were rolled up to his ankles and suspenders dangled at his waist. His plaid shirt was buttoned halfway up, his gray-haired covered chest clearly visible.

From the dank hallway came a raspy, early morning voice, "John, why you up so early?"

"Those Rebs came through once without a fuss. I'm gonna be ready for them next time."

"Well, John Burns, don't you beat all. You are entirely way too old to be doin' any kind of fightin'. You fought in 1812. You fought in Mexico. You got nuthin to prove."

"Im'ma not provin' a thing to nobody, nohow. I love this house and I love this town. Im'ma gonna defend things I love. That means you too, Mrs. Burns," retorted John sarcastically.

His wife huffed through her nose, blowing out the hot steam of frustration. John sat up from the chair, rungs rubbing against slots, and stepped outside into the humid morning air. His eye lids closed partially and he inhaled deeply while his brain began to deviate; wondering what would come next.

"They's comin back," he spoke softly aloud, "I hope them Culp boys aren't around here. Their daddy will sure be torn, one fightin for us and one for them. But…"

"John, come in for some breakfast."

"Cummin'," he yelled back. He turned towards the house putting his hand on the door knob, but turned his head to the west. The ominous sky began to tell its story of the coming rain and destruction. "Yup. They's a cummin'

Chapter Two

Habakkuk 1:5

*Look at the nations and watch— and be utterly amazed.
For I am going to do something in your days
that you would not believe,
even if you were told.*

June 30, 1863

Joshua could feel the pulsating blister on his big toe leaking liquid into his sock. Looking back at his platoon he winced a little in pain, then reluctantly put his left foot up into the stirrup and climbed aboard.

"How fer we goin', sir?"

"Until we're commanded to stop, Private Walker," he replied with a smirk.

Chuckling a bit, Walker replied, "I got that much, sir. But where we gonna get to?"

"Well, I assume we're trying to be at Gettysburg, but you know how valuable real information is in the Army."

"Yes, sir. We tend to move on rumors," said the middle-aged private. "Thank you kindly, Lieutenant. The boys 'n me just trying to hear some skinny."

Chapter Two

"Uh-huh."

"Josh!" someone shouted, interrupting the private's next thought. "Oh, sorry Private Walker."

"It's fine Lieutenant Perry. I was wanderin' my way back anyways," said Walker, slowly backing his way into his unit.

"What's wrong Nathan?"

"Hey! We known each other since we was little, Josh. Why all of a sudden you callin' me by my full name?"

"Sorry Nate. Thought maybe of keeping it official after Chancellorsville. I've only been at this lieutenant thing for a month now."

"Well, quit it. Makes me squeamish."

Emphasizing the need to move the conversation, Joshua stressed, "Anyway Nate...."

"Oh, yeah! I just got yelled at by Colonel Fry."

"That's nothin' new. You always get yelled at by our commanding officer."

"I guess it's no different with this one too." Nate chuckled to himself as he gazed off.

Bringing him back to the present, Joshua laughed, "Hey, what did he yell at you fer?"

"Oh, he said I was a der-i-li-ctin...um...my duties. Said I wasn't managin' my platoon right."

"What'd you say?"

"All I could say, 'Yes sir, No sir' and then moved on."

"Typical Nate Perry. Sarcastically agree and hope the big wigs don't realize it."

"Yup!" the toothy grinning Perry chimed.

"Suppose you should get back to your platoon so's you don't get yelled at again."

"That'd probably be good, huh?"

"Yeah," Joshua whispered.

"Well, I bid you ado and farewell!"

Violently Joshua exhaled and shook his head as Nate turned his horse to meet back up with his platoon. Anderson shifted in his saddle, pushing down on his right stirrup to straighten it out. He chuckled a little after thinking about his friend, a small sardonic grin flashing across his face.

The men walked with weary steps, letting their confabulations overtake their blistered feet. Their minds wandered to talk of home, the rolling green hills, the rows of knee-high corn and the similarities of this countryside to their own. The sight of cattle in a fenced-in field drew their attention and the Blue Ridge Mountains behind them caused more conversations. Gray, red and brown barns littered the countryside, while the subtle smell of pine trees and manure filled their nostrils.

Joshua overheard the men talking about families and friends, fallen or alive, and about sweethearts. He was perfectly content with keeping to himself, silently discussing things within his own mind. He thought of his own farm while looking at the plush green grass surrounding him. It brought back memories of his family and how much he missed them and how much guilt he felt for leaving.

"Lieutenant, flankers have reported in," someone interrupted his guilty thoughts.

Shaking off the remorse, Joshua replied, "Go on."

"They report no enemy but only healthy farms, sir. We gonna eat good tonight."

"Tell 'em to leave something for these people. We gotta be better than them Yanks. Tell 'em to remember Fredericksburg."

"Yes, sir," replied the messenger, spurring his horse and riding off.

The heaviness loomed, held pendulously in the air, a feeling of wrongness or a sentiment of battle. Joshua could not distinguish if he felt unfavorably because they were marauders in this peaceful province or felt uneasy being in enemy country. He inhaled deeply, releasing the hot breath of unrest, shaking the feeling from his brain.

Chapter Two

The formation of marching men advanced upon a light gray house, the blue shutters closed, a small brass band playing Dixie in the front yard. Meanwhile, an old hunched over man, heavy gray beard on his face, stood glowering at them. No smile passed his countenance, just a grimace and a simper on his lips. A cold chill went down Joshua's spine, forcing him to sit up straight in the saddle.

As they passed by the jubilant Army band, no handkerchiefs were waved, no small flags hung outside windows and no one vociferating their acclamation to the men. There was only the lone man staring at them through small wire framed glasses. A triumphal passing it was not, but Joshua held fast in his saddle, not looking back at the man.

"Whoo wee, that man sure didn't like us," exclaimed Private Walker.

"Sure didn't," replied Joshua, dismounting his horse, enabling him to walk next to Walker.

"But I don't understand these Yanks anyway. They always bein' uptight and all. They don't know how to relax. Take that gent for a second. I betcha he ain't sat down since Pettigrew passed by," Walker laughed loudly. "Prolly has a stick up his backside keepin' him up straight."

Joshua smirked from the corner of his mouth, but uttered no words to encourage the talk.

"I mean, why they fightin' anyway? What've we bin doin' that harms 'em? Always buttin' in where theys don't belong, tryin' to tell others how to live. Just let men live. It don't matter anyway. Next time we see 'ol Hooker, he'll run agin. Them blue bellies always run."

"You think so Bill?"

"I know so. They always run. Those blue bellies got nothin' to fight for, no reason to shoot at us."

"Perhaps. But they sure do send a lot of men to die for nothin' then. Wonder what God thinks of all this killin?"

"Hmm. I don't know much about that. We all got our own reason for fightin'. I certainly got mine," Walker said looking to the tree line on his left.

"What's that, Private?"

"Me!"

"Hmm?"

"My name. My daddy's name. My momma's name."

"I don't understand."

"My pa fought in 1812 with President Jackson down in Louisiana. I weren't being thought of back then. Got lost in them woods down there. They thought he deserted and wanted him dead, but Jackson had mercy. Just banded him out. Went and settled in Alabama, had me a couple years later."

"So you got somethin' to prove?" a puzzled Joshua shook his head.

"Yup. I got to prove daddy's honor. I fought back in Mexico, that wasn't enough. Maybe now."

"I hadn't heard any of those things. I mean, you know, being from Alabama and all, thought maybe…"

Walker cut him off. "Sir. I keep it wrapped up. Hope you will too."

"I will Private. My word is honor."

"Much obliged sir. I'll be headin' back to my ranks now," Walker exhaled wearily. "Thanks for listenin'."

Joshua continued walking on the left side of his horse, reflecting on Walker's story and his comment of everyone having their own reason for fighting. Walker's reason was family honor. What was his? He owned no slaves, had no qualms about the North, only that he didn't like them as the pragmatics they were. What was his reason?

Again, he removed a rag from his left pants pocket and dabbed his forehead, wiping the sweat. "Dang hot," he commented to himself.

"Sir?"

Chapter Two

Looking behind him, Joshua answered, "What is it Sergeant Horton?"

"We lost a man," the sergeant stated softly, his head held low.

"What?" Joshua's head tilted, brows scrunched together, "Who? When?"

"Corporal Yeager just fell out."

"Keep the platoon moving. I'll have a look," Joshua stated as he handed the reins of his horse to Horton and began walking back down the road. "Private Walker, come with me!" he shouted to his comrade.

The platoon and regiment streamed by them as they walked in the opposite direction. Feet scuffed the gravel, boots crunched on the dirt and horse hooves thudded on the ground causing soft thundering in their ears. Walker and Anderson stepped up to two men from the platoon who were standing over Corporal Yeager.

"Thank you for standing by, catch up with the platoon," ordered Joshua. *Lord, please be with us* he silently prayed while kneeling to take a look at him. "Walker, go get the doctor, he's still breathing."

"Lemons. I see lemons!" yelled a delusional Yeager. His breathing was erratic, fitful inhaling met with intermittent exhales. Shivering as if chilled from the cold though the heat was a vehement degree, caused everyone to be miserable. It made Joshua think of how General Jackson would suck on lemons.

Private Walker returned, a doctor right on his heels. "Open his shirt, take out a rag and canteen."

Joshua complied. The doctor kneeled on both knees and touched Yeager's chest. "His skin is clammy, he's got down from heat," the doctor stated. "He's extremely hot! Heart is beating faster than horses' hooves at a race."

Pouring water from the canteen onto the rag, he placed it back on the corporal's head. Yeager's eyes rolled to the back of his head, his eyelids then closed and his body began to quiver. "Oh Lord," whispered Joshua.

Corporal Yeager began to tremble violently, his whole body shaking, moving him around. His head bobbed up and down, vigorously striking the grass on the side of the road. All the three men could do was watch impotently as the young man lay succumbing to the heat. As soon as the seizure began it stopped. Joshua waited for it to start again, but it didn't.

The doctor felt the man's throat, and lifted his lids to look into his closed eyes. "He's gone," the doctor stated while standing to his feet. He tipped his hat and walked away leaving Private Walker and Lieutenant Anderson alone. Neither of the two spoke for a minute or two, the silence overcoming both of them.

Kneeling back down he marked Yeager's body.

"Whatcha doin?" asked Walker.

"Makin' sure the burial squad behind us knows who he is."

"His ma ain't gonna be pleased."

"Whose mother ever is?"

"I mean him being buried up here!"

"Oh."

"He was a good kid. Listened to older folks, followed us that knew something'."

"I feel we grow to love it…at least be accustomed to it."

With a quizzical look on his face, Walker asked, "What's that sir?"

"Killin'…death," whispered Joshua. He cleared his throat. "Let's get back to the platoon."

They climbed the small acclivity of the ditch, making their way back to the road. Filtering their way through a column of soldiers they doubled their pace to make it back in front of the regiment. The hearts of both men were held in lamentable suspension as their feet drudgingly took them to their platoon in front of the boisterous, stentorian line of the

Chapter Two

13th Alabama. The morale of men was high in spirit and quite girded for action, lifting Joshua's own soul.

Father God, he prayed silently, *I thank you for these good men. They are solid and true just as you are faithful to these that believe in Your Son.* His prayer was cut off when he reached his horse and the line was slowing down.

"Why we stoppin'?" he asked.

"Don't know. Some kind of hold-up," replied Sergeant Horton.

Pulling out his pocket watch he looked at the time. "It's a little after noon."

"Wonder where the front of the column is?" questioned Walker.

"Probably near Gettysburg by now."

"Maybe that's why we stopped," remarked Horton.

"Don't know." Joshua was about to say more when a man approached him from the leading columns.

"Lieutenant, turn your men around. Move back toward Cashtown."

"Whose orders are those?" he queried.

"General Pettigrew."

Col. Fry returned to the front of the regiment. "What is going on here?"

"General Pettigrew says to turn back," answered Joshua.

"Why?"

"Don't know."

The messenger spoke up. "General Pettigrew says he saw Federal Cavalry in Gettysburg."

"How in God's name....alright, let's turn this regiment around. I just returned from General Archer and then this. Lieutenant, stay with your platoon. Perform an about face and keep your men moving. I'm going up to herd this regiment back."

Joshua mounted his nervous horse which was tapping her hooves on the ground. "Platoon!" he yelled while kicking his mount's ribs, moving to the rear of the platoon which now became the front. "We're moving back to Cashtown. Now turn about and keep this line moving!"

An anxious sentiment fell over the men, their stomachs tingled with acid and their breathing became heavier in the heated afternoon. A formidable feeling inched its way into their psyche, controlling their movement. Each soldier began to bump and stumble into each other.

The mass confusion caused heads to tilt, brows to crease and choleric words to be passed from one to another. The men could feel the additives mix together, that of unbearably humid heat and a looming battle that slowly assaulted their spirits. Desperation invariably set in.

"I said form up! One at a time. Take your time, settle down now! Move forward." The men began to respond to the verbose directions. "That's it! Move out!" In a circular motion, Joshua slashed through the air, putting an imaginary gash in the atmosphere with his sabre.

The line moved back from where they came, while Walker approached. "Whatcha think, sir?"

"Don't know."

"I mean about Federal Cavalry?"

"Don't know. I know that Pettigrew ain't some career soldier. I know he's an anxious man, heard he always paces."

"You think he's wrong?"

Joshua shrugged before putting the sword away. "I just don't know Bill, I don't know."

The regiment came upon the old man's house they had passed by previously that day. There he stood, still hunched but with no band playing behind him. A small smirk came across his face, a look of causticity that cut Anderson's esteem. *You like seeing us fall back don't cha old man,* he thought to himself. *Oh don't worry now. We'll be back. Count on it. We will return to your town!*

Chapter Three

◆

Revelations 22:3

Behold, I am coming soon!

June 30, 1863

James' body began to relax, his muscles easing from the tension of the many days the unit had been riding. It seemed as though every morning he would wake to his body screaming discourteously to his brain that getting out of bed was foolish. Captain Spalding straightened his right foot by pulling it out of the stirrup. Rotating his ankle and bending his knee, he attempted to remove the rigidity of riding.

A lieutenant rode next to him, a loquacious man but still a good friend to James and one of the platoon leaders. He didn't hear much of what the man was saying as his mind drifted off toward his wife's last letter. Her last three words worried him; *please come home.* She wrote how she was ready for the baby to arrive, her disquieted feelings of child birth. The mood of the letter had switched from nervousness to hatred. Hatred of the war and the desire for it to be over no matter which side won. Closing his eyes, he again thought of her words. Sighing he opened them.

"Knock it off, Jim!"

"Hmm?"

"Stop thinking about your wife," the lieutenant said.

"I was not thinking…." he began.

"Don't lie to me. We have been friends for a long time. We grew up in Rochester, played by the river and married sisters. I know you!"

"Yeah..well, Matt. You are right," stumbled Jim.

"I know I am. Look. Julie is fine. Her letter just was telling you how much she missed you. That's it. Try not to read too much into it. Barbara is there, our mother-in-law is there. She's fine."

"I suppose."

"Hey, you remember that time by Wilson's store? You know when we threw that crate in front of that buggy?"

James began to laugh. "Oh yeah and you blamed me for the apples tipping out of the back."

"I never thought you would ever get to come back out and play."

"Pa was sure mad at me. But not as mad as when you threw that rock through our window."

Matt wailed out a laugh. "Oh I though your pa was going to kill me. Never been yelled at quite like that before. Scared me half to death."

"Lieutenant Clark?" a corporal interrupted.

"Yes Corporal."

"Private King isn't feeling well."

"I will be right there," responded Matt as the corporal turned his horse around and trotted away. "Well Jim, I'll see you in a bit."

"Alright, Matt."

James looked to his right and noticed two rocky hills, the right one bigger than the left. He began to think; his brain trying to picture the maps in his saddle bags. His memory wasn't serving him well, as he couldn't remember the names

Chapter Three

of the hills. A peach orchard and wheat field enveloped his eyes as he began to really take notice of the landscape that surrounded him; two long ridges on either side of the Emmetsburg Road. Rolling green hills, small ponds that seemed to just materialize, queues of trees hiding their secret of the wide open fields behind their plump green leaves and thick brown trunks.

Through the clamor of horses and equipment mingling together in a barrage of clangs, claps and jingles, came a bugle call. James pulled back upon the reins, bringing his horse to a halt while he held his right arm up in the air, the forearm and bicep bending at a 90 degree angle. The company behind him stopped as did the whole division.

"What's this about?" asked a trooper.

Remaining silent, he just shrugged his shoulders, while listening for another bugle to sound off. For several minutes the only noises to be heard were the men talking, the humid breeze wafting through the trees and the anxiousness of their heartbeats. Horse hooves broke through these quiet noises as James watched a rider approach the middle of the column.

"Captain Spalding!" yelled the messenger.

"Yes? Right here."

"Oh...Yes, sir. Colonel Gamble wants you. Follow me, sir."

"Lead on Lieutenant," James turned and left a subordinate officer in charge and spurred his house following the messenger.

Captain Spalding followed pace at a gallop, his horse kicking up sod as they moved. He inched his way next to the messenger and asked him, "Where is Colonel Gamble?"

"He's at the front of the column with General Buford. They're near a cemetery outside Gettysburg."

"What is going on exactly? Why have we stopped?"

"You'll find out, sir. Easier to see than to explain."

"Understood." His thoughts began to race, all firing at one another. *What could be so important he needs my maps? Maybe we're lost or perhaps Buford forgot what I had shown him earlier. I guess it will be revealed in God's time anyway,* he thought.

Ahead he could see Colonel Gamble and General Buford, both dismounted, the colonel wiping his nose with a handkerchief. Buford stood, looking through binoculars. After reaching them, James waited for a moment watching Buford just standing there like a statue, his lips mute.

"Captain, bring your maps to me," Buford said breaking the tightly glued seal of his mouth.

"Yes, sir," he replied and grabbed the mane of the horse with his right hand, his left remaining on the reins. Pulling the right foot from the stirrup, he swung his leg around the rear of the mount, disembarking from his ride. The brown leather squawked and moaned from the motion as he moved to his saddle bags, lifting the folded papers.

James walked over to a rock that was nearby and lay out the maps. "Where does Emmetsburg Road take us?" asked Buford.

"Well, sir," he replied tracing his ungloved finger on the paper, "it takes us into town and then that leads to any direction you want."

"Hmm."

"What are ya thinkin?" asked Gamble, his Irish accent still in his speech.

"Jim..what road leads west?"

"Two of them, sir. The Hagerstown Road and the Chambersburg Pike. The Mummasburg Road leads northwest..."

"They're on the Chambersburg Pike. Good. They could get bottled up there. Keep 'em on one road," replied Buford.

"Who, sir?" asked James.

"The rebs," stated the general.

Chapter Three

"What...," Buford handed the looking glass to James and he placed the lenses to his eyes. A nervous acid built up in his stomach as he prayed silently. "Sir, they are turning around."

"They're not to have contact," said Gamble.

"Must be," said Buford. "Nonetheless they know we're here. They will be back, most likely in the morning."

"How do you know that, sir?"

"I feel it in my gut. They're Lee's men marching down that road. Jim, Lee can read a map better than you can make 'em. They're not coming back for us they're coming back for this town, for their water...for their ground." Buford began to rant. "They'll march through...all mighty and proud, beating their chests like baboons and squawking like Indians. Lee will have his men march down from the North and converge on this town like a mountain lion on its prey."

"Sir...," James tried to speak but could not. Buford was too deep in thought to hear him.

No one spoke, not truly knowing what to reply. No words could articulate the feeling they had within their hearts.

"Gentlemen, it's now noon," Buford stated as he replaced his watch back into his jacket pocket. He sighed heavily before barking out his orders. "Move the men into town and conduct *will* be strict. We're not here to socialize. Colonel Gamble and Captain Spalding come with me. We're going to have a look around."

"Yes, sir," they replied in unison.

They mounted their horses and passed instructions to each regimental commander, the word spreading down the line that the Confederacy had been located. With each passing message the enemy grew, the enemy became more grandiose. While the information was passed from man to man, the anxiousness and bewilderment grew; that wondering feeling of life or death, safety or carnage, wholeness or disunion of a nation. The three men left the division and made their way to the ridge southwest of Gettysburg, heading to a steeple hanging in the western horizon.

The cupola stood like a star, guiding the men, leading Buford, Gamble and Spalding to a place of contemplation. It felt as though this tower was a small glimmer of hope, a small portion of faith sent from heaven. James felt a tug in his spirit, a nudge of boisterous empowerment from God. A sigh of relief blew out from his hot, suspense filled lungs as they approached what they now saw was a Lutheran Seminary.

"Let's go up top," cracked Buford, "bring your maps, Jim."

James responded by saying nothing but climbed off his horse and wielding the topographical charts that had been strapped in the saddle bags. The men walked up the front steps of the seminary and Jim knocked on the door. The response was an eerie silence that chilled them in the humidity of the noon day sun. The closed shutters and bolted windows told the story of a town that was scared, torn asunder by the ravages of people whom they once called brothers. Their fears were legitimate and concerns now made pristine clear to the three men.

"Open it," commanded Gamble.

"Yes, sir," James replied as he pulled his pistol out and pushed open the door. He quickly scanned around to see if any souls, enemies or friends, were in the building. With his pistol leading the way, a small sweat bead rolled down his forehead into his eye. Batting his eyelids and breathing heavily, he waved his hand to indicate that it was safe to enter.

They found the steps that led to the cupola and ascended them, pushing the hatch to reveal the platform at the top. Buford stood in the covered area for a moment, a deep silence on his lips and heavy somber thoughts in his mind. He broke the silence after a few moments.

Chapter Three

"Gentlemen," he began, his western accent on his breath. "I haven't much cared for a lot of command decisions of late, but do you fully grasp the situation?"

"Yes, sir, I believe we do," replied Gamble.

"Good, 'cause we're going to fight tomorrow. You know what happens if we hold this ground for Reynolds and his corps?"

"Sir, we may win?" James rhetorically answered.

"We have a better chance. Do you know what happens if we lose?" Buford asked gazing off to the Blue Ridge Mountains in the western sky. Neither man answered him. "The mothers of the dead are crying gentlemen. The fatherless children and widows are weeping, weeping for us to win. If we lose, they'll march on Washington, overrun it and besiege the president calling for an end."

Buford continued. "The wide open fields of death that have caused mountains of bodies and seas of blood have to end. Our families will only suffer so much. If we lose gentlemen…we forfeit our nation… we forfeit our ancestors… we forfeit our lives. The fate rests solely on us. On our shoulders. Our fate rests solely upon the eastern sun."

Silence lay upon their mouths, heaving on their hearts and discombobulating their minds. *Our fate rests solely on the One who raises the sun in the east*, thought James.

Buford pointed to the west. "Right there," he said, his fingers extended to a group of trees along the Chambersburg Pike. "We will make our stand there. Along the fence row, along that beautifully laid ground. The small bluff can oversee the enemy approach. The woods can block some advancement of the Rebs. Where are your maps, Jim?"

"Right here, sir," he replied, unfolding and holding the maps with both hands, arms extended out.

"Fine. Look here Colonel Gamble. Put your brigade here, stretching from Mummasburg to Hagerstown, across that railroad cut there. Put Colonel Devin up on these northern roads that meet, the uh…Carlisle Road. He can look and report any enemy coming down from Carlisle."

"Sir what about the roads east of Gettysburg," asked James.

"Lee doesn't have any troops that far east, at least last scouting puts it like that. It's difficult with Stuart out there, lurking about. Colonel Gamble, I want pickets out in front of your brigade. I also want Calef's batteries up on that road. Take care of it," said Buford.

"Consider it done, sir."

James folded the land charts, the paper crinkling and snapping as the creases bent. He stuffed them into his satchel which swung from his shoulders. The men climbed down from the cupola, exited the seminary and mounted their horses. Their heels tapped the ribs, the powerful legs of the rugged but elegant animals moved, the reins leading them into town where the division was held.

They entered town, riding on the empty streets, hooves clopping on the hardened road. The townspeople watched, scowls slowly turning to stone faces as some women waved handkerchiefs, the men glared. "Them rebs already raided our homes, our shoe factory," one angry citizen shouted.

"General, I do not understand. They are all upset with us," James softly spoke.

"The men are mad because we weren't here to stop the rebs and the women are in fact happy because…well we're here. War is a curious thing, Jim."

"I will not ever understand it."

"Only two kinds of people do. The insane and the dead."

The two brigades of cavalry gathered their supplies and began to pack up, moving westward out of town. The townspeople stood in bewilderment, their army moving out, their protectors leaving them. They stood on the porches or sat on their front steps. Old men leaned up against walls of brick buildings, their hands in their pockets or clasping their pipes.

Chapter Three

The ladies stood properly at the windows of homes. Some with tear filled eyes fully realizing the totality of the circumstance, they absolute reality of what was about to happen.

Children were on the street curbs, within sight of nervous mothers. They shouted at the troopers, "Hey mister, hey soldier!," hoping to get a treasure or trinket from the knapsacks. The soldiers looked at the faces of each man, woman and child while the eyes of the people returned the gaze. Each taking mental pictures to remember the protector or the protected.

The sounds of boots and hooves on cobblestone streets echoed through the alleys and crevices between buildings. The citizens listened to the unsettling clamor as tin mess kits, cups and metal struck against each other. Sabers rubbed on brass buckles and rifles hit creaking leather straps. It was purely a sight out of a book; a surreal slow motion event. They felt as if it were something they had just read about, but had never seen. Now it was real, now it was real life brought to their porches and screened doors.

These sights and sounds continued for almost two hours as James and the rest of the cavalry moved west of town. He was with his men at a fence row with others from the 8th New York. They reinforced their defensive positions with rocks, planks of wood and leftover railroad ties. Cannons, wheeled into position, remained mute, only to speak when spoken to.

Captain Spalding approached Colonel Gamble who was delivering orders to Lieutenant Marcellus Jones of the 8th Illinois. He waited for them to be done but Colonel Gamble interrupted himself by addressing James, "Ah Captain, I have been looking for you."

"Sir?"

"I have a letter for you here. It was delivered special, I guess some sort of emergency."

"Thank you, sir. But while I have your attention, I would like to volunteer for picket duty sir."

"Jim, I have already chosen Lieutenant Jones here and his men…"

Interrupting, James replied, "Sir, I will adhere to what he says."

"I suppose. Fine. If the lieutenant has no objections?," Gamble looked to Jones who nodded his head, yet a frown crept on his lips. "Then it's settled, you will move out with him. But get back as soon as you make contact, double time yourself back to your maps."

"Yes, sir," James replied and saluted while turning to leave. He almost had forgotten about the letter until reaching half way back to his company. Stopping in mid-step, he pulled the envelope out from his left tunic pocket. Breathing heavily, he just stared at the name on the paper. He had known it was from his wife, but was preoccupied with the preparations of battle. He gently ripped the back of the envelope, slipped the paper out and began to read.

My dearest James,

I am writing this letter not only to say how much I adore and love you but to tell you we now have a beautiful baby girl. She has your blue eyes and your nose. Eightpounds of pure beauty. I will write more later, but I must get back to our child. I am devoted to you and my heart is yours.

Your loving wife,
Louise

"I told you she'd be fine," a voice interrupted his thoughts.

James turned and saw his friend and brother-in-law Matt. He wiped his eyes. "Yup."

"Come here buddy," drawing him in an embrace. "Congratulations Jim. I am happy for both of you."

"Guess that makes you an uncle now," he sniffed, chuckling as he remarked.

Chapter Three

"Yeah, I guess so," Matt quipped back as he handed James a cigar.

"Do not say anything to anybody, please Matt."

"Why?"

"Just…well.. it's complicated. Just keep it to yourself."

"Fine," the puzzled man replied.

"Captain Spalding," interrupted Lieutenant Jones, "We are moving out."

Matt looked questioningly at James, "What's going on Jim? Where are you going?"

"Picket line."

"What!" yelled Matt. "Jim…"

Sternly interrupting, James looked at his brother-in-law, "I will have no debate." With that he left Matt looking stunned, mounted his horse and moved out with Jones and the others from Indiana.

They slowly rode out onto the Chambersburg Pike, the setting sun hanging just over the Blue Ridge Mountains. The colors of summer (yellow, bright orange and fiery red) mixed in a collage of awe inducing illumination. The horizon seemed to be in a balance of day and night, an illusion of a struggle of light and dark.

The morning was surely coming, but what it brought neither side could foresee. What the day would entail was in God's hands. A day of prayer, a day of faith and most assuredly a day on which all days would lean upon. For the morning would not be just another day, it would be *the* day.

As that day turned from evening and evening to night another new day slowly crept in like a thief in the night. It was to be the end of one day and the end of a month. It was a new beginning for so many and yet an uneasy feeling befell him. A feeling of indefinite end, a thought of darkness, a sense he had never felt before or ever wanted to feel again. The thickness of night drew heavy on Gettysburg and the outskirts of town. He hoped to wake in the morning, hoped the enemy would not come, just simply hoped and trusted in God that he would have the chance to see his daughter.

James leaned up against the bough of a tree, kneading the letter between his fingers, a small smirk upon his face. His eyes glazed over as he stared at the paper, focusing on the envelope. He continued to look at it until night overtook him and he could see no more.

Chapter Four

Psalm 17:11

They have tracked me down, they now surround me, with my eyes alert, to throw me to the ground.

Army of the Potomac

June 30, 1863

A light rain battered the roof of the cupola above Buford's head. It lightly tapped the covering as if light fingers were monotonously rapping their sporadic rhythm upon the surface. The general's eyelids were half parted as the day's heat and continuous activity wore his energy down to nothing. He looked to the west, across the dark expansion and could only see rows of campfires off in the distance and fireflies dancing in the obscurity of night. The two visions mixed together in an array of light that caused Buford's lashes to bat as he attempted to focus.

He put a pipe to his mouth, his finger caressing the glossy brown wood and with the other hand, lit it with a match. Sucking in, the sweet tobacco tantalized his nose and began to scratch at the surface of weariness. Buford focused on his letter to General Reynolds of First Corp and spoke briefly upon the dire situation that was facing him in the morning and almost was forced into mendacity, asking for infantry support. He yelled for his aide, but Lieutenant Jerome, Buford's signal officer, came running up the steps.

"You call for someone sir?" asked Lieutenant Brainard Jerome.

"Yes Lieutenant Jerome. I was calling for my aide," replied Buford, rubbing his eyes.

"He is asleep sir. What can I do for you?"

"I need a courier to take this to First Corp."

"I would be honored to take it to a courier sir."

"Thank you Brainard. That would be wonderful."

"Yes sir," replied Lieutenant Jerome and he stepped downward toward the main floors of the seminary. Buford rose to his feet, walked around the circular floor of the cupola and rested his arms on the railing between the vertically arched banisters.

He looked to the darkened east, his eyes seeing nothing upon the landscape and the moon clearly hidden by the overcast of the late night hour. General Buford's heart sank for a moment as the darkness closed in, realizing what his decision actually meant. He decided to keep his men on an outnumbered battlefield with only darkness behind them, only a dark eastern sky.

The vision that flashed in his brain became painfully clear, so translucent it might have been from a mountain spring. He could see his men running through the streets, toward the hills blocked out by the night. He could see President Lincoln sign the defeat papers; General Meade hand over his sword. Buford saw the clear result if his men did not win here, did not hold this ground. But... what if they did?

The general rose to attention as the thought struck his brain. What if they won? How long could this war endure?

Chapter Four

He now saw visions of bloody streams and floating bodies all flowing toward an open sea of death. How many more must die? "How many men will I kill?" Buford spoke aloud.

He walked back around to the west and looked upon all the fires again. His eyes were heavy, saddles of war cinched to them. The general's mind told him to sleep, his body called to him for rest and he decided to listen. His feet took him to the steps without thought, but he stopped at the first step and looked once more the east before heading down.

Once on the main floor of the seminary, Buford removed his overcoat and set it on a chair. He laid down and rested his head on his saddle, crossing his ankles he closed his eyes. The problems were laid before him preventing his mind from shutting down with the biggest uncertainty being the lack of answers.

****

Meade paced the ground, the grass matting down from his steps. The tent was lit up by a multitude of lamps, his silhouette easily observed from outside, it moving back and forth. "I must have information."

"Sir you need to rest, it is well after midnight."

Meade mumbled a curse.

"Sir?"

"Nothing. Where is Reynolds? Buford's up there trying to fight the whole Confederate Army," yelled Meade, cursing a little once again. "I must know where all the pieces are. I do not like to move without knowing how it will work."

Meade's aide spoke meekly, "Perhaps it is best to just move on faith sometimes sir."

"What?"

"Nothing sir." He hung his head.

"Fetch General Butterfield for me. Perhaps my chief of staff will have some information."

"Right away sir." The aide left the tent with a sense of relief to get away from the onslaught of nervous energy, leaving the flap swinging from his exit.

The silence of loneliness rose from the grass slowly inching its way to the peak of the tent and into Meade's ears. He ceased his pacing and stood for a moment staring at the side of his sloped walls before sitting down in a wooden folding chair. A long febriled sigh passed from his mouth as his hand rose to the sweat ridden forehead. Meade rubbed slowly but passionately with his fingers, kneading the skin and pressing on the temples.

The crickets outside spoke to the few that were inside the tent. Their conversation carried on as though no war was tearing apart their habitat and land. The nervous acid in the general's stomach seemed to be in agreement with the tone being used by the loudly chirping crickets. Both gave the distinct impression of pending doom, or so it appeared to Meade.

"General Meade!" the aide yelled from outside the tent.

"Enter George."

"Sir. General Butterfield had bedded down …"

"Why did you not wake him ?" yelled General Meade.

His son continued as if not interrupted, "...but received a little correspondence from General Reynolds. He is on his way."

"Finally... some news."

****

The man sat at his desk one hand writing on paper, the other twirling a ring on a chain, dangling from his neck, between his thumb and forefinger. His mind was on the papers in front of him, orders and requests from I Corps, but an interruption brought his brain from them.

Chapter Four

"A courier sir," came the voice from outside his tent. He stood, reaching his hand above his head stretching then bringing them down he brushed his tunic, straightening the wrinkles. He adorned his hat and brought his trim, lanky body from within the tent. A horseman stood there breathing heavily. "General Reynolds. A dispatch from General Buford."

"Thank you trooper," replied Reynolds receiving the note. "Captain, get this man a chair for a moment so he can rest, and some water as well." Reynolds turned to the opening of his tent to read the note by the lamps that were lit in the entryway.

General Reynolds,
 Have located Reb army just east of Cashtown. I have good ground to defend small town of Gettysburg. Please come at all possible speed. Will hold until you arrive.
J.N.O. Buford.

Reynolds took a brief moment to write a response back before quickly turning to the messenger who was sitting down regaining his composure.

"You have ridden hard son. This information I am giving you must be ridden with equal rigor. Take this directly to General Buford and give him my compliments, we will be there in the morning."

"Yes sir," came the reply. The trooper mounted and kicked his horse off into the dark night the sound of the hooves slowly dying.

Turning to his aide, Reynolds made a drinking motion with his hand. "Could you get me some coffee Joseph?"

"In this heat sir?"

"Could prove to be a long night... please."

"Yes, sir."

General Reynolds stepped back inside his tent, rubbing his neatly trimmed beard with his hands. Four fingers brushed the right cheek, the thumb hitting the mustache and palm lightly covering his mouth. The general stared at the map of Pennsylvania laying unfolded on his large wooden desk. He didn't need to, he knew the area, but still continued to gaze at it. Reynolds pictured the landscape in his mind. Closing his eyes he remembered the cool autumn breeze that blew through the trees the last time he had been in the area.

Allowing his mind to deviate once more, he thought back to Catherine Hewitt, back to his love. He pulled the chain out and thumbed the smooth ring, slowly raising it to his lips and gently kissing the precious metal. Eyes closed and heart open he pictured the love and affection of a woman who returned the same adoration. They might have been from different backgrounds but the general didn't care though as he pictured her face and tried to feel her lips pressed against his once more...

"Coffee sir!"

Reynolds cleared his throat. "Thank you Joseph."

"Anything else sir?"

"No...oh... um... wait yes. Please inform General Meredith to get his brigade moving in the morning. Have them move out early."

"Yes sir."

Reynolds was once again alone and he noticed the gold ring was still outside his tunic. His cheeks flushed a little and he embarrassingly put the chain underneath his shirt. Sitting at his desk he began writing a message to General Meade, the pen grasped between the fingers ready to write. His mind began to go blank, the fingers just holding the writing instrument, no words forming. He placed the pen back into the ink and stood from his chair. The message was too important to write.

Chapter Four

General Reynolds walked to the flap of his tent and pushed it back, stepping out into the early morning darkness. He gazed up the Corps, upon his command that lay out in the deep black night. Only campfires and lamps suggested their existence, only small sporadic conversations gave away the position of human life within the dismal night tide.

He mounted his horse and a short time later was at General Meade's headquarters. Inside, the old man was pacing nervously as Reynolds explained everything he knew and had commanded. Meade grunted and nodded, but remained silent for the majority of the meeting. At the end of General Reynolds' briefing, Meade finally spoke. "We will concentrate at Gettysburg. Thank you John. It is not what I wanted but... perhaps it will..." the general trailed off.

Reynolds nodded his head. "We will know more upon the rising sun sir."

****

Army of Northern Virginia

June 30, 1863

General Heth sat at the fire, listening and watching as the wood crackled. It snapped and popped as the ballet of flames dances to the symphony of the wood. He was staring, absolutely riveting upon it in an abstraction state. No thoughts were coursing through his brain, no idea running lucid. He simply sat there staring at the flames.

"Eh-hem... General Heth sir."

"Hmm...oh... what is it Corporal?"

"A message from General Hill sir," the corporal said while handing him the message.

General Heth,

Move into town the town of Gettysburg in the morning. There have been reports of cavalry in the area, but believe is it is just militia. However, there is to be no contact, from General Lee, no action. Will further instruct upon occupation of town.

General A.P. Hill

"Tell General Hill that I have received the orders and understand them," stated Heth. "Oh.. and give him my compliments."

"Yes, sir."

Heth watched the young man return to his horse and ride away, once again leaving the general to his fire. He wasn't as transfixed this time; he thought of movements and the heat, General Hill and command. A nervous feeling began to swelter inside the pit of his stomach, wondered if "Little Powell" or General Hill and General Ewell could fill the boots of Jackson. Heth began to think briefly upon the dead, the mounting names that he knew or didn't know. He closed his eyes wishing that he could open them and be home. But he opened them to the very same fire that seemed to be haunting him.

The general began meditating on General Hill, a unique man yet brilliant in his own right. He would wear a red shirt into battle and use trickery as a weapon. Jackson always said the best way to fight a war was "mystery". Heth believed that Hill used this to his advantage at Sharpsburg. Bravery was nothing new to Hill, but yet would become enigmatically ill before a battle after taking command of a portion of Jackson's corps. He didn't like to think poorly of his boyhood friend and groomsman.

Various amounts of thoughts began to exude from his brain and formed a great measure of mental images. From

Chapter Four

Ewell's lost leg, to his bald head. Then he shifted back to Jackson and began to smirk about Jackson sucking on lemons, or how he would not use pepper for fear that it would give him pains in his leg. He would take naps before a battle and start messages, "through God's blessing..."

Heth's eyes filled with water thinking about the day he heard the young boy yell out, "Jackson's dead." He cursorily shook his head to sift the thoughts from his mind. Standing and inhaling deeply, he walked to his tent and entered with a hand grasping a wooden post, his fingers brushing the coarse wood ever so softly.

"Still too big sir?"

"Huh? Oh, no corporal. Didn't realize you were back, you startled me."

"Sorry sir. Your hat fit then sir?"

"Yes, yes. I think the foolscap that quartermaster put in it did the job rightly. Cannot believe that it took a dozen sheets but all is well," replied Heth.

"You need anything before I bed down sir?"

"No...no. I think everything is in order. Oh, there is one thing son. Could you please send word to General Archer to get his brigade out first thing in the morning. I don't expect too much resistance. Artillery in front in order to show militia strength in power."

"Yes sir."

The corporal exited the tent and the general removed his coat, slinging it over a chair then sitting down onto his cot before removing his boots. Small grunts and groans came forth when laying on his back. Exhaling a long hot breath he stared at the dimly lit peak of his tent. His mind took him back to Virginia, back to his wife, retroceding to simpler times. As his eyes closed he saw her kneading dough to make bread, saw himself sitting at the table watching. The gleam of his eyes, the love of his wife, he was home, if only for a minute.

****

Johnston Pettigrew paced inside his tent, tenderly rubbing his neck. He stalked the ground with an antagonistic attitude, the grass below him trodden down with repetition. "I know what I saw," he said aloud. His right fist pounded into his left palm. The unlit cigar pressed between his lips softened with the wetness of his mouth, the pursed lips scrunching the tobacco slightly.

Pettigrew's aides said nothing to him, leaving him to be with his thoughts and brooding emotions.

Chapter Five

◆

Joel 2:2

"A day of darkness and gloom, a day of clouds and blackness. Like dawn spreading across the mountains a large and mighty army comes…"

July 1, 1863

"No sense in sleepin with this heat," Joshua whispered to himself. The heat plagued everything that breathed in the air of life. It was violent and tormenting, as if the coals of Hades had come to this Pennsylvania countryside. The heat struck each man, but it wasn't what was keeping him awake. The ominous feeling of impending gloom clung to his shoulders, cloaked him in the bubbly acid of his galvanic stomach.

Joshua rolled onto his stomach, slowly rising to his knees, eventually working to ascent from his wool blanket that lay upon the ground. He turned his head left and right, observing the rest of the army. The majority slumbered uncomfortably upon the earth, the fires that burned vigorously the night before were reduced to embers. Joshua walked over to a tree with a low hanging branch and grasped it with his hands, stretching his arms. A twig snapped behind him and he turned quickly.

"My apologies lieutenant. I didn't mean to startle you."

"Colonel Fry. No sir, you're quite alright."

"I saw you were up, appears to be only us right now."

"Yes sir."

"General Archer has given the order to strike camp and move out. We will be the lead division and our regiment will be out in front, well sort of. Our artillery will be out in front of us."

"Sir?"

Fry sipped from his coffee cup. "Yeah. All fifteen of them."

"Crazy sir... my apologies sir. I didn't mean to question."

"Quite alright Anderson," replied the colonel.

"Are the rumors true sir? Cavalry in Gettysburg?"

"I don't think so... General Heth doesn't think so if you can tell that," Fry stated referring to the artillery being in front.

"What was all that commotion yesterday then?"

"Who knows. We've had units all around this area. Probably just locals stirring up suspicions, making us wonder about it."

"Maybe..." trailed off Joshua.

"Well... listen lieutenant. I'll leave you to it. Get your platoon moving. I'm going to find your company commander. Get this regiment moving."

"Yes sir."

Fry moved away from Joshua, leaving him alone with the heat, crickets, and butterflies in his stomach. The sense of morning began to ease off his mind as the fog dwindled, being replaced by coursing thoughts. *Today could be a boring day if they're right. What if they're wrong though?* He shook his head to whisk his thoughts away.

Chapter Five

His eyes went to the hardened ground below him and he knelt to his knees. "Father," he whispered aloud. "Keep us safe this day. Let us not forget our ways and our cause. No matter the outcome of this day, fight or not, remember my men Dearest Father. Remember all their sacrifice… remember their courage God. Let us not falter in our duty, let us not fail in our objective. And Lord, this may be selfish but please give word from home. Don't let the enemy ransack it too much. Amen."

He rose, performing an about face, moving toward his platoon sergeant. "Baker…" the man continued to sleep, only slid his legs slightly. "Baker… Sergeant!"

"Hmm…"

"On your feet. We're moving out," called out Joshua.

The sergeant inhaled deeply and exhaled saying, "Ok." Joshua remained quiet for a moment. "Oh! Yes sir. Sorry Lieutenant."

"Quite alright. Let's get movin' though. We have a full day ahead of us."

Going back to his own blanket, Joshua began to gather his belongings. He meticulously placed a picture of his family in his rucksack, his fingers gently caressing the fulminate paper. He rolled his blanket up and wrapped it around his shoulders, before strapping on his black leather belt on which contained his ammunition pouch and sword. The gold buckle snapped through the punched holes, the leather creaking and popping as he did so.

"Sir the platoon is 'bout up and ready," proclaimed Baker.

"Good, good. I will be there in a moment to address them. The regiment cook is… well should be done. We'll get some food then move out."

"Where we headin' lieutenant?" asked Baker.

"Gettysburg."

"Hmm… thought there was suppose be enemy about there?"

"Army rumors? Your guess is as good as mine."

"Yes sir. We'll be ready rightly so."

"Very well."

He stood there for a moment and took in the sight that always amazed him; a sight that caused his spine to have a trickle down chilled feeling. A grandiose, eye awakening event that occurred whenever the army moved. Men working in groups to tear down tents, wagons being loaded, weapons slung over shoulders and eyes being rubbed red to awake to another day. Coffee would steam from cups, meat slightly charring on a flame and arms stretching high into the air distending the muscles.

Joshua approached his platoon, each man leaning upon a tree, their muskets, or each other. Their weary eyes told the story of an absolute exhaustion that words could not bring validity to explicate. They teetered, nearly toppling to the ground, their legs still not awake to the new day. He looked at each man, rubbed his dark brown beard and nodded his head slightly.

"We're movin outta here in a few. I know we marched a ways yesterday… but we're um… we're goin' back to Gettysburg today. Our regiment will be the first in line of this division… well, sort of," Joshua smirked. "We will fall in right ahead of the whole regiment, but behind our artillery.

I don't rightly know what we gonna see today. There were reports of cavalry, Yankee cavalry. But… them reports have changed to militia. Either way… be alert. We could have a fight up comin' here real soon. I don't much expect sumpin today, but who knows. If we see them Yanks, let's give them a true Alabama welcome." Some toothy grins and tobacco spits accompanied his words. "Alright let's fall in and… Godspeed men."

Chapter Five

Muskets began to be draped over shoulders, hats placed on heads and the feet of every man shuffled his way to his place in the formation. Joshua walked over to an aide who was brushing a horse, the brush moving in a circular motion. The blacksmith was well awake, pounding his heavy instruments against the anvil. "Is my horse prepared?" asked Joshua.

"Umm.... Sir... the, well your horse is gone," replied the aide.

"What?" shouted Joshua. "What do you mean gone?"

"The cavalry needed it."

"Excuse me. You mean to tell me my personal horse that I brought from home was taken from me by our own country?"

"Yes sir. They uh... left this though."

Joshua grabbed the paper in the boy's hand. "A promissory note to pay me from the Confederate Army?"

"Yes sir, I'm sorry..." He turned and left the boy in mid sentence.

"Sir any order?" asked the sergeant, running up to meet him.

"They took my horse Bill. You believe that!"

"Sir?"

"Nevermind. Those...God help me. Anyway, make sure that the men have plenty of water. It's another hot one and with this marchin' we'll soon be parched. No one leaves without a full canteen of water."

"Yes sir. Sorry 'bout your horse."

"Hum."

Joshua walked up a small embankment to the column of men that were formed on the road. Looking ahead of him he saw the artillery beginning to move, the large spoke wheels slowly creaking before rolling away. The caissons rattled with the cargo it contained while the wooden lids knocked like rapid reiterative knuckles on a front door. He walked to the head of the line, behind his company commander and Colonel Fry, positioning himself within his platoon. All of the legs began to drudgingly move upon the command to march, as they moved out in the early morning darkness in late afternoon-like heat.

Bugles blew in the distance, while the sound of flags gently rippled in the breeze. Their mouths remained closed from lassitude, but their feet moved from the repeated ordered inclination and each head seemed to heavily lay fallen toward the ground. Joshua's angered march led him down the road, his mind beginning to wonder in the early morning air.

As his thoughts became like the rushing rapids of a river, his shoulders began to carry more than the burden of war or weight of equipment. They yoked themselves with the emotions of memories of a life almost forgotten. Joshua went back to Alabama while his exasperated thoughts brought him to his horse. He closed his eyes only briefly but the images caused it to feel eternal, while he pictured the day his mother gave him the horse. This rumination brought forth his sister, then left him feeling suddenly cooled, the anger turning to sorrow allowing his eyes to open, wondering why he wasn't there.

Reality spun back into focus quickly as the sounds of the army returned to him. Men began talking more as their bodies became more awake. Metal would jingle, leather creak, tin clink and hooves clop on the hardened dirt beneath their feet. Each step would produce a noise, each movement causing a chain reaction of reverberating din that lifted high into the humid air before being choked out by distance, wind or trees.

"Sir…"

"Hmm?"

"This heat… you think we'd be use to it but I'm tellin ya, I don't think a man ever gets use to it," said Walker.

Chapter Five

"If a man ever says he's use to this kind of weather he's a liar, or… lived in a swamp his whole life."

Walker began to chuckle. "Had an uncle, marched with my daddy down in Louisiana. Stayed there afterwards. It was the funniest thing. He said the climate fit 'em just fine."

"Can't see how."

"Me neither, I think it was some witch lady that he fell in love with. That or the gators he loved."

"How could you love a gator?" asked Joshua, shifting his belt, pulling it up on his hips more.

"Makes money. Hunts 'em, sells 'em. Things like that."

"I'll stick to my farm. It's a bit safer."

"Not so much now with them bluebellies…" Walker stopped himself.

"Yeah," exhaled Joshua.

"…or a plow goes nuts cause of a horse," Walker inserted.

Joshua began to chuckle. "That happened to Nate one time." His chuckle turned to laughter. "He tried to get the back field done by himself and in some sort of record time. So anyway, he's a whipping this horse, making him work real hard."

"Why's he tryin' to get done so fast?"

"Something about a card game… I'm not sure, he's Nate. Anyways, he gets this horse all worked up. So it takes off on him. Nate tries to jump away from the plow, but doesn't realize his foot is caught on a leather strap. So here's this horse runnin, plow is fumbling all over and Nate two feet behind the plow foot in air body dragging on the ground."

Walker began to laugh. "Lucky he wasn't killed."

"Oh… the man is clumsy but his luck is not denied," Anderson stopped talking and noticed Walker limping. "What's wrong?"

"Nothin' sir. Just my feet. Nothin' to be alarmed 'bout."

"You have no shoes."

"Haven't for a while. Hoping to get some in Gettysburg, heard something about a factory."

"Move off to the side." The two men moved off to the side of the road while the regiment continued by them with shuffling feet and crunching gravel. Anderson removed his belt and overcoat setting them on the ground. "Give me your bayonet and sit down," Walker complied and Joshua took the stabbing tool, tearing a piece of his shirt.

"Oh, no sir. Not the shirt offin' your own back."

"We do what we do."

"Yes sir."

Joshua cut an equal length of cloth off both sleeves and smiled at Walker. "No sense looking like I have one sleeve. Besides, it's a might cooler now." He took the left foot in his hand first and winced. Walker's feet were dirt ridden from the ground but sliced wide open. The blood that had been draining mixed with the dirt to cause a caked on mud like substance. Any sore that had possibly been there was now torn open, oozing out a discolored white puss. "Walker, you'll need attention."

"Just wrap 'em sir."

"There is no need to do this. Just from walking and being here this long… you've restored the name."

Walker leaned in a little and said to Joshua, "Honor is restored only when I say it is. Now sir, please just wrap 'em."

Joshua began to wrap Walker's feet, encircling the foot with the cloth before tying it into a knot. He repeated the steps for the next foot before replacing his coat and belt. "I will find a wagon for you to ride on."

"I will walk sir."

Joshua exhaled loudly, "Very well then, let's move out."

The two men quickened their pace to get back to the front of the column. Anderson squinted his eyes not only from the sun that was beaming its rays down upon them, but also from the dust that was being kicked into the air. The rain

Chapter Five

seemed to just soak into the ground not preventing the dirt from being dried out. Joshua noticed the beards of each man had a grayish color that seemed to emanate from his face. He wondered if his own beard looked like that. Running his hand through his beard and looking at it gave him the answer he had thought. *The dirt gets everywhere.*

They returned to their platoon as it was beginning to pass in front of the aged man's house they had gone by in the previous day's march. Joshua half expected the man to be out in front again but he was not. He looked around while still marching, his head moving up and down. The man couldn't be found, and he noticed the house was shut up tight. The windows with the shutters closed, the white wooden gate was shut and through the window on the door no light could be seen.

Joshua turned his head away, eyes facing forward once again, his brows scrunched together. He felt it was a prognostic warning of trouble ahead; a haunting feeling came over him sending a slight glacier chill down his spine. His breathing became slightly heavier as he closed his eyes to regain his composure, allowing the noise of the army to engulf him, allowing the din to swim though his ears and remind him of their strength.

What was it that drove them? What was it that drove so many armies to storm the castles and fortifications? How did David fear not the giant? Joshua looked around at his men, exhaustion and weariness seen on the wrinkles on the sides of their eyes and yet they were driven. As the armies of David fought for the Lord, these men too fought for something bigger than each of them. They fought for something that was not seen, something that hands could not feel and tongues could not taste. It was a cause in each of their own hearts, in their spirit that pushed them past where ordinary men would faint and even extraordinary men would pause.

Joshua could not shake this feeling of obscurity, the feeling that something sinister laid ahead of them. It was the kind of pathos that sent men's stomachs to their throats and hearts to their feet. When telling of this feeling around the fire, men would call it the feelings of heroes, but when faced with this in reality, it's called fear. A fear of which he had never known and wasn't able to understand. He could only relate it to walking into a dark and damp room being alone, with the absolute understanding there was no one else to turn to but God, and it felt as if even He were silent.

The sun was rising over the eastern sky producing the heat of a thousand demons from hell. His rag was already soaked with sweat and did nothing to relieve him of the dampness upon his forehead. Joshua looked ahead of his platoon and saw the caissons rolling, their lids jiggling and bobbing rapidly up and down from the road. The cannons ahead of them were being pulled by teams of horses, their long black barrels angled downward toward the dirt below. He pulled out his watch and noticed it was a little after seven in the morning. Clicking the clasp closed and returning the gold time device back to his pocket, Joshua looked up once again and saw the tree line in front of them flash and the sound like that of ears of corn in a fire.

The head of one of the canoneers flew back and a red mist spurt into the air, then another fell to the ground soon after.

"Contact, we have contact!" a rebel yelled out.

"Forward men, forward!" another screamed.

"Corporal, go and tell General Archer that we have contacted the militiamen that was reported yesterday," barked out Fry.

"Sir, we don't yet know who is in front of us," cried out Joshua.

"If I wanted your opinion Lieutenant I would have asked you directly."

Chapter Five

"Yes sir."

The canons moved to the side allowing the infantry to pass by them. Joshua quickened his pace along with his company, each foot passing incessantly in front of the other. His chest rose rapidly from the breath being taken from him by his stamina decreasing every second. Joshua stared intensely at the trees ahead of him and watched the men jumping down from trees and mounting horses. The blue uniforms in front of him caused his eyes to open a little more, his retinas responding. One of the canoneers with a musket fired at the blue uniforms, the blue body flailing through the air, finally the body falling to the ground.

The fifteen canons moved into a field just beyond the trees, unhitching the canons from the horses, moving the caissons to the rear of the instruments of destruction. They set their wheels and distance before opening up the mouths of death. The guns inaugurated their fraction of the battle with rings of smoke bellowing out the ends. Their lead balls rained down on a line of enemy crouching behind a fence and stone wall. Joshua's men looked ahead to the axis of blue in front of them, but was unable to move towards it because of the fenced in Chambersburg Pike.

A few men began to dismantle the wooden structure and throw the pieces down in the field to the left. The opening that appeared was small, but enough that Joshua and his platoon were able to cascade through it. As they entered the shin high grass that was before them, Joshua formed the men into their battle lines. His sword was drawn from the scabbard, pointing in the direction he wanted the soldiers to be placed. More of the fence row was dismembered and a multifarious amount of men entered the field, lining up to march into battle.

"Form up men, form up," yelled Joshua. His heart began to beat in a cadence that mirrored a drum line and gave the demeanor of being just as loud. His hand shook from his adrenal gland pumping profusely, and the flight response caterwauled to have him leave, but his patriotism jostled him forward. Joshua's feet felt as if they were encased in brick, the heaviness of each step taking a little bit more energy from within him.

The men of the 13th Alabama moved at first in disarrayed movement, before their feet appeared to move in the rhythm of each other. The only break in the walking was when the sporadic rifle fire from the fence and wall ahead of them would bring someone to his knees before he fell to his face, seemingly disappearing in the tall grass. A round screamed past Joshua's head and he flinched just for a moment, before looking behind him and noticing that it had landed in the chest of one of his men. Turning his head from the grisly scene, he once again focused on the small knoll in front of him.

The men marched forward into the fray of bullets and death, not wanting the man beside him to see their own fear. The apprehension each man felt coursed through his veins just as the blood was pumping through it. Without the understanding, without the knowledge of love each man could not have pushed his way through the fear and continued to move. It was not love of state or country that urged them forward, but it was for the love of the man next to them. The bullets that streamed past one and inserted their hellish heat of death into another only fed the appetite within their stomachs to not founder the conscript to the left and right.

Joshua reached the middle of the small knoll of which they were fighting to gain and stopped his line. As the commands of make ready sluiced down the Confederate line, the shaky muskets were pulled off of nervous shoulders. Before Joshua could give the order to raise the wooden instruments of projectile death, the blue line exploded open with a blinding and suffocating array of blazing fury.

Chapter Six

1ˢᵗ Corinthians 13:11

When I was a child, I talked like a child, I thought like a child, I reasoned like a child. When I became a man, I put childish ways behind me.

July 1, 1863

He threw another log on the fire it crackled and hissed at him as he did so. She patted the ground next to her, the long flowing nightgown ruffled around her ankles. She offered to read to him, offered to soothe his heart with a passage. He couldn't stop looking at her dark hair and the cheek structure. Her bones positioned in just the right place, just so that it caused him to shiver. He lifted his hand to stroke her hair....

"Captain? Captain, it is almost dawn sir."

He awoke with a start, kicking his legs into the muck beneath him.

"What? What did you say Corporal?"

"I said is almost dawn sir. You said to be awakened. Lieutenant Jones is already awake."

"Yes. Very good. Thank you."

"Yes, sir."

The corporal ran off down the line with his rifle in tow. James smirked to himself, not fully knowing who the corporal was, and of course it didn't really matter. They all wore blue, and in this present moment on the picket line, nothing else was of much significance. He rolled his head, attempting to work out the kinks from the night of using a tree root for a pillow. Remaining in his seated position, he yawned heavily before reaching into his tunic and pulling out the letter from the night before.

The sun was not yet out, and the words were not yet visible but it didn't matter. James smiled a toothy boy like grin. He closed his eyes and lifted his hands to heaven. "Thank you God." His soul was in peace and at that moment, in the tranquility of the morning air, there was peace.

"Captain."

"Hmm."

"Lieutenant Jones sent me down to give word. Daylight is approaching fast. We need to make ready."

"Thank you."

Reality settled upon his shoulders once again. Taking a deep breath, James let out the hot air through his nose. The humidity and brashness of the air caused his nerves to be a little unsettled and his eyelids to become heavy once again. He dreamed of home, the river behind his home. But something was wrong, the river flowed freely but the water was no longer the crisp fresh scent that permeated into the air. The water was now blood. Along with the streaming of it came fresh body parts, arms, legs and screaming faces frozen in time. His leg kicked out and woke him with a startle. Within an instant his pleasurable thought of the inconsequential and peaceful had turned to deep short breaths of a nightmare.

The sun was newly-established within the atmosphere allowing James to retrieve his gold timepiece from its resting place. In the distance he could hear a drum rolling off and

Chapter Six

the sound of which took his eyes from the timepiece making them dart to the horizon in the west.

"Sir, would the general's engineer care to have a piece of bread. It could be a very long morning?" asked the lieutenant from Illinois.

"Thank you."

"I do not understand why you chose to be out here sir."

"I love the mornings, the dawn of day where things are fresh."

"Sir?"

"I have no idea why I came out here. I told myself it was to count the battle flags and give a report to General Buford but now... I am not quite sure. As I turn behind me and see the sun rising over blackness of night, I am reminded of how much I have always loved the dawn."

"Forgive me sir, I am not following."

"Look at the sky, the haze of heat aside, it is truly beautiful. I wonder what I am doing here... then again why we are all here. I wanted to get into the battle but now... I apologize I am not making sense."

"No sir, then again not much makes sense these days. I'm a long way from Illinois."

"Hmm. It sort of feels like home here. I have not travelled far from home myself and this is the longest time I've been separated from my family but then again...," James trailed off.

"Yes."

"When we look at what we've shared over these few months. I don't know, it feels like this fight that is coming in force down that road is bigger than all of us."

"Sir, it *is* bigger than all of us, in fact it might kill all of us, and for what? A few darkies?"

"No... more than just that. All of war is glorified by parades and stories from people who have never seen it, like myself. Perhaps that's why I am standing here in these woods with you at this very moment. God and country has nothing to do with why we stand in a line and butcher one another. 'Our freedom is not in jeopardy, why do we fight?' many ask. Preservation of land? I do not care one bit about preservation or the fact that this president of ours has asked me to do so. I joined at first because I wanted respect and dignity. But after living the sort of life that a soldier lives, I see that there is not a shred of dignity left within me. I guess that is what God wanted to show me. I fight to see another dawn…".

The silence between them was interrupted by the sound of wagons rolling along the dusty road. "Cannons?" questioned the lieutenant. "That's odd. Prepare to fire and move out, pass the word," he whispered.

Men wiggled around the equipment on their bodies, the leather straps creaking and moaning with anticipation… Jones picked his borrowed weapon up and set his sights on the lead cannon… he breathed heavily his chest rising and sinking… he stopped and held his breath… slowly, pulsating index finger squeezing the trigger… the world lit.

"Move back to the line…"

Horses and men became a convoluted mess of traffic of the Chambersburg Pike, as they spurred their horses toward the line. Wind blew in James' face, the mustache riotously waving and catching the dirt from the horses in front of him. The blond hair curling around his ear flapped, tickling the lobe, his hat fully drawn over his scalp to prevent it from blowing away.

The horses passed Buford's line as Calef's Battery was beginning to prepare their cannons. James high kicked his leg over the horse's head and leapt to the ground, passing the horse off to a handler.

Finding Gamble passing orders amongst the fray of men he reported in, "Sir a division." Gamble just squinted his eyes, wiped his nose and nodded.

Chapter Six

"Stay in the back until a hole appears in the line, then plug it," commanded Gamble. "I do not know how much hell I will be catching for allowing one of the general's engineer's to fight but we need everything we can get."

"Sir," James saluted and ran to a spot near a cache pile.

Calef's Battery opened fire on the road ahead of them, the dirt flying through the air as the ball of destruction met its target. The rebels broke through on the fence line surrounding the road and poured into the field in front of their line. That awful squelch arose in the humid air and lingered in his ear… the line opened up with a stream of consecutive fire… the order to fire at will given… soon the line began to spew red and holes began to form. "Captain, get in there."

He went to get up, but his legs wouldn't move and seemed to stiffen from the idea of running to the line. "Captain!!!" Someone handed him a carbine… breathing became thicker…hands trembling… legs finally moving. He seemed to be out of body while running as if it wasn't really him pushing to the line.

He reached the line and sighted his rifle upon the soldiers ahead of him, pulling back on the trigger he shook all over. A returned piece of lead struck the man next to him in the shoulder, the blood splattering over James' face. "Captain, pull that man to the rear." Harnessing the man's leather straps around his body, he drug him away.

A scream from the air and a light from the ground… the deafening sound resonated within the hallow darkness of his brain. Darkness trembles…

Chapter Seven

Psalm 27:3

*Though an host should encamp against me,
my heart shall not fear:
though war should rise against me,
in this will I be confident.*

July 1, 1863

General Heth awoke well before the sun peaked its rays over the horizon. It did not take him long to dress and be about quickly, ready for the day. He picked up the picture of his wife on the desk, kissed it and returned it to its place. Heth stepped outside his tent and donned his sheet filled hat. He felt foolish having picked the hat, especially since it did not fit his head. The quartermaster quickly fixed it with some paper, but still it felt foolish. The General adjusted the hat and inhaled the warm morning air, letting out a large breath. He looked to the dark sky and felt a cool mist fall upon his face. He said a small prayer and looked over to his adjunct, still asleep.

"Ah, to be young," he thought aloud. He looked at his aide, not wanting to wake him yet. It might prove to be a long

Chapter Seven

day. The boys would need their rest. General Heth began to think on the youthfulness of the days gone by. Images of his home and his time at West Point filled his mind. He saw his jubilant cousin, George Pickett and of course his wedding day. To be young and wistful, full of pride in the uniform.

The present day came back to him and he looked at his watch. Very early, but the General wanted to get moving. He moved over to the young adjunct and softly kicked his feet.

"Awaken, young man, the day is upon us," the General said.

"Yes, sir!" the young man said, smacking his lips still very sleepy. "Oh...um...Yes, sir!"

He quickly rose to his feet and saluted. "I'm quite sorry, sir. It is I who should be calling upon you. I apologize."

"No, no. I heard you up late last night discussing.... strategy."

"Um..."

"Poker strategy, but strategy nonetheless. Well, Major, let us look to this day. Get the men up, get them moving."

"Yes, sir!" The young man slipped his boots on and was quickly off heading about his business.

Heth inhaled the hot air and shook his head. *This stifling heat,"* he thought. *Even though the light has not shown its head, it is daunting.* The lungs in his chest filled with hot humid oxygen. Feeling as though it burned he exhaled a hot breath. "I could heat my coffee with this," he chuckled. Looking at the dark liquid in his tin cup it rippled and swirled for him, mesmerizing his thoughts. The man's perfectly placed mustache could be seen in the reflection in the mug, his wedding flashed through his mind once again and he longed for her embrace and sweet whispering lips speaking to his ear. *I miss you,* he thought. *I will make you proud.*

****

He was well awake before dawn. Buford peered off into the darkness, puffing on his pipe and blowing the smoke into the wind. His eyes squinted as he looked into the distance. As his horse slowly made its way west on the Chambersburg Pike, Colonel Devin cautiously rode up behind.

"Sir, I am not intruding am I?" Devin asked.

"Not 'tall, Colonel."

"Sir, my regiment is up and ready for the day. We are in place north of town per your instruction."

"Very well, Colonel. We shall see how the day goes."

"Sir, the troopers are ready for a fight."

"I know that, but at what cost? We have good ground, but I fear maybe I have made a mistake to stay and fight. Reynolds is a distance off and this action could prove to be fated for us," said Buford.

"Sir, we will hold, no doubt to it. We have held before."

Buford didn't speak, just looked off into the darkness. After a short silence Devin spoke. "Well, sir, I will go about the day's business." Devin went to leave but turned, "Sir, we have to hold this ground. We have to hold it to win it."

With that, Devin left Buford to his thoughts as he rode toward the line of blue and dismounted. He woke Colonel Gamble and they began to wake the boys one by one. Tired, restless bodies awoke and began to eat and drink their coffee.

Buford climbed the steps of the cupola, pushed open the hatch and rested at the top. He sat there and looked toward the dark western sky. A small rain began to fall upon the roof. He listened to the drops of rain fall, one plop after another. He closed his eyes remembering the rain hitting his roof out west. No sound in the world could match that of tiny little rain drops on a roof. It was the sound of safety, security and simpler times.

His eyes opened to a small bit of daylight creeping its rays out of the east and breaking through the clouds. He turned his body around to look at the sunrise. Orange and

Chapter Seven

yellow filled his eyes, causing his pupils to dilate and his lids to squint. Taking one last puff on his pipe, he cleaned its contents and returned it to his pocket. He inhaled a long breath and held it, then slowly released it.

Pop! Pop! He heard several shots ring out of the morning air filling his ears with that unmistakable sound of musket fire. He shot off the bench and looked out across the open fields in front of the seminary. The blue lines of troops were scrambling, getting ready for the brawl. He lifted his glasses to his eyes and looked. He could see Captain Spalding return with the scouting party. The reports would soon rain in, replacing those drops on the roof that were now subsiding.

The first report came in. According to battle flags, there was a division. Heth's division, if the reports of regiments were correct. Buford mustered a smile. Good ground and he's sending a division. He liked the thought of it. The cannons began to open fire and he saw what looked like lightning bolts dart across the sky. It was not from the heavens, but artillery raining down on the enemy.

General Buford wrote out a report and gave it to an aide. "Ride out to General Reynolds. Tell him to come as quickly as possible!"

"Yes, sir," the boy saluting as he ran off.

"Well, gentlemen, we have a fight on our hands," Buford said aloud.

The enemy was now out in front of the long blue line and coming forward when he heard the high pitched yell, like that of the Indians out west. The rebel yell. He saw the butternut uniforms run forward into a hailstorm of bullets, then quickly fall back.

"They are falling back, sir!" an aide said excitedly.

"Not for long, gentlemen. They will be back. I am going down to the line."

Quickly descending the staircase, he almost glided down them. Buford mounted his horse and spurred him. The horse responded to the urgent message and moved forward toward the line. Directing his horse to the line of battle, Buford was greeted by Gamble.

"Sir, we got 'em runnin' fast!" yelled Colonel Gamble.

"Good. Fine." Replied Buford.

"Sir, our losses are minimal, head and shoulder wounds. Only...if they come at us in any force they could overwhelm our position."

"I know. I know." Buford said, "I will pull some of Devin's boys off their line to reinforce you."

****

The late morning hours found the sun shining brightly. It beat down on the elegant man's face as he put his hand to his chest and felt the ring around his neck. General Reynolds cocked the left side of his cheek in a half smile as he remembered her.

The general loved to ride horses and was quite good at it as well. Every so often he enjoyed riding alone; today was one of those times. Being there was a fight ahead he was deep in thought. He rode out in front of the First Corp along with the rest of his belongings. His corp, with the black hats of the Iron Brigade, stretched out fifteen miles behind Reynolds and behind them was the Eleventh Corp. Twenty thousand men in all.

General Reynolds thought on the position he was offered and why he had turned it down. Although being commander of the Army of the Potomac had a nice sound to it, he could not accept. The President and too many Generals had their hands in this war. Too many politicians telling soldiers what to do. The only way to win a war was to have good strategy and fight. There was no time for discussion, no time at all. Get good ground, draw the enemy in and fight!

Chapter Seven

The General shook his head and thought on Meade, the new commanding officer of the army. Some things bothered Reynolds about Meade. He was overly cautious, having councils of war to make decisions. He may be brilliant but sometimes being brilliant and being dumb was a fine line. The other factor that made Reynolds question Meade was he was not American. Sure he lived in America and commanded here, but Meade was actually born in Spain. The only good thing was he had moved to Pennsylvania. This means he should know the terrain and its advantages.

His thoughts were interrupted when a courier came galloping up in front of him.

"General Reynolds, I have a report from General Buford, sir."

"Give it here son," Reynolds said with hand extended. He opened the note and read.

General Reynolds,
Enemy has attacked in force west of Gettysburg. Only one division as of yet. Lee has the main body coming down the Chambersburg Pike and am pretty sure coming down from Carlisle. Am holding as of right now. Status of your situation is requested.

"Major, ride back as quick as you can and tell General Buford to hold. We are well on our way and should be there in two to three hours. Tell him to hold for us. And he should be commended. Repeat that back to me, son."

The major did so and rode off hard into the distance while Reynolds returned to his men.

"Well, gentlemen, we have a fight on our hands. Tell all regiment commanders to keep their men moving. We must make it to Gettysburg very soon."

The aides saluted and moved off into the dust. Once again General Reynolds was deep in thought. He lifted his head to the sky and said a quick silent prayer. *Let this war be over soon. Reunite us with our loved ones and reunite this county. It is in your hands and I leave my soul into you, Oh Lord. Amen.*

Reynolds began to think on the country and its states. This country had been torn apart, well before the war broke out. Many debates were circulating before 1858 brought controversial decisions, including the Dedd Scott decision. Buchanan was more afraid of losing his power and sorting his niece's mail than uniting this country. One catastrophe after another appeared and he sat in office doing nothing. Then the Presidential election brought us Abraham Lincoln. This started the war.

He had never really thought much about the commander in chief. He knew Lincoln was a radical Republican and most army officers were Democrats. The south despised this man, but what did he really want? What were the intentions of this President? The questions filled his head yet no answers appeared. Only one thing could the General think; to do one's duty. Command and lead these boys. That was the only thing to do. Lead them so perhaps many could live to see their families again.

Looking to the sky, Reynolds lifted the boys to God. The First Corp was almost to Gettysburg and he heard the sound of cannons off in the distance. The General began to feel that familiar feeling in his gut again. That feeling. That knowledge of combat. The knowledge that death was to become many a young man in the hours ahead. He felt the ring on the chain against his chest.

"Lead us into the fray, Lord. And lead us from the battle intact."

****

Chapter Seven

Johnston Pettigrew rode next to General Heth, the horses moving steadily but with just enough hesitation to not make if feel as though the world was swashing by.

"The problem with running a country, no matter which country it might be, is the government itself," said Pettigrew. His left hand motioning around in a circular motion, signifying the entirety of the world, "When the government becomes large, the people are the ones who suffer."

"Hmm," replied Heth.

"Every system, every person has their flaws but it is due to the human aspect of life."

Thunder began to rumble in the distance.

"General," began Heth. "Is that thunder I hear?"

"Certainly sounds like it sir."

"Curious."

Again it sounded... then again.

"That is cannon fire General," said Heth.

"Yes, sir."

"Get your men up to the front, I'm riding up there." Pettigrew pulled back on the reins and turned his horse around while Heth looked to the front of the line hoping it was just militia.

****

"I know what the report says but I want confirmation from Reynolds. He is out in the front," bellowed General Meade, cursing a bit.

"Sir, this is from General Reynolds. He indicates that General Buford's calvary has been attacked west of ...um... Gettysburg." said the young captain.

"Well is this the way it is going to be? I have yet to call a council for my generals. I do not even know what kind of forces I have or how big the enemy is. How am I to run this army if generals go off and start battles without orders?"

"Sir, Reynolds said he will be on the field within the hour, if not already, sir. I am sure that General Buford is holding strong. There is good ground. That is the rumor, sir."

"Rumors. I am to move on rumors!" screamed Meade. "What kind of army is this anyway? Very well Captain, inform General Reynolds the army is coming and I will be there by nightfall."

"Yes, sir."

Meade strode off into his tent and gathered his hat. He yelled for his son and told him to strike camp and to bring up his things. He was going to ride ahead to attempt to establish command.

"Son, also tell Hancock that when he gets there he is in command. Tell him to take command immediately and establish a headquarters."

"Yes, sir," his son said as he ran off to follow the directive.

Meade was now able to think a little more. He attempted to clear his mind to think on where to position the army, that was if he had an army. Perhaps the enemy was greater or maybe less in number. That was what troubled Meade, he wanted to move slower, not to be drawn into action too quickly. He wanted to position the army on good ground. He didn't want to be like his predecessor and get the army divided.

Endless thoughts flooded his mind. Between that and the heat he felt drained, exhausted. He closed his dark eyes and let the horse carry him. He almost drifted off but his aides woke him in the saddle. Reports were now flooding in, a flood like Noah's. He answered them one by one, getting more irritated by each question, each report. Then came a report from Washington.

"Sir. I have a...."

"Yes, yes, everyone does. Read it quickly," Meade yelled interrupting the man.

"Sir. I cannot. It is from the President!"

Chapter Seven

Meade took the sheet of paper and read it.

General Meade.
As new commander of this great Army of the Potomac, I understand and duly note that it will take time to adjust. Unfortunately, there is not time. The enemy is now in our country. Pursue and destroy them as quickly as possible. Abraham Lincoln.

Meade pocketed the paper and looked at his aide. He said nothing only thought to himself. Thinking on how to carry out the President's orders, on how to do it quickly. No answers came, no special formulas. The equation came to a question mark, came to an x but he couldn't find what x stood for. Mystery. All a mystery.

"God help us!" Meade blurted out then muttered a curse.

Other reports came in and General Meade went about business knowing the enemy was out there. Sensing the Confederate victory was close and hoping he could stop them, he hoped that he was not the man by whom they would gain their independence. Hope! It was all he had.

Chapter Eight

2 Kings 3: 18,19

And this is a simple matter in the sight of the Lord; He will also deliver the Moabites into your hand. Also you shall attack every fortified city and every choice city and shall cut down every good tree and stop up every spring of water and ruin every good piece of land with stones.

July 1, 1863

"Fire!"

Joshua had his sword high above his head, shouting, yelling commands at his men. "Reload boys, quickly boys!" Moving back and forth pulling men up from the rear to fill the line, file closers. Bullets and minie balls were screaming past him, whizzing through the air. Men were falling everywhere, one after the other. The Union was keeping up a hot stream of fire.

He could hear the enemy's rounds hit people, breaking through the flesh and crunching the bones inside. It was a sickly sound and had taken a few battles to get use to. Anderson looked up upon the hill and saw the long blue line

Chapter Eight

of cavalry continue their fire. The order came to fall back and he barked out the order.

"Fall back boys, follow me, fall back!"

The men of his platoon fell back while still firing at the long blue line of troops. His platoon, as well as the rest of the regiment kept falling at a rapid pace. Out in an open field in plain view of the enemy was not good ground, not the best position for battle. As he fell back he could see Colonel Fry yelling at the rest of the regiment.

The platoon moved back away from the smoke, but the sound of cannon fire continued. The Union would fire, then the Confederate would answer. The men of Joshua's platoon were reloading, jamming their minie balls down the barrel then cramming the ramrod down the long shaft. They were breathing heard, battle and heat caused some to fall due to exhaustion.

"Listen, when we go back let us move a little closer in order to get a better shot at the enemy. We push them off that hill, we take the town!" said Joshua.

"Sir, how they shooting so much?" someone asked.

"They musta got them new carbine!" another yelled.

Taking a drink of water from his canteen, Joshua gulped down the warm liquid. The temperature didn't matter, he swashed it around for a short second in his mouth and swallowed. It drained down the back of his throat and made its way to his stomach. It refreshed him just enough before the orders to move forward once again came down the line.

The clatter of steel rods falling back to their resting places resonated through the air. Men yelling over cannon fire and the cries of the wounded caused a frenzy their hearts echoed throughout the smoky humid air. Musket fire, screams, orders being given. It all went into the air with the smoke and fog of battle. Joshua looked around and could see death and destruction.

The order was given to advance and he gathered his platoon and fell back into the battle line. They slowly made their way through the tall grass toward the killing fields west of Gettysburg. They came atop a hill and the whizzing of bullets reverberated in the eardrums of the men.

The Union continued to fire into the Rebels. Many men falling in front of Joshua who was still filling the holes but now was running out of men. The gap began to grow, to be too much. He moved his men forward even more and gave the order to stop and make ready to fire. The men lifted their muskets, barrels facing toward the enemy. Once again he commanded his platoon to fire and the muzzles flared to life, projectiles flying forward. The bullets flew through the air and found targets in heads and shoulders peering over the fence line. Anderson could see spurts of blood fly into the air.

"Reload boys, reload!" he yelled, trying to contend with the cannons and muskets. The fog of war was heavy and it began to get hard to see the enemy at times. A small breeze came and visibility was somewhat restored, a small gift from God within the carnage. The men reloaded within minutes, all while the Union shot at them.

"Pour into 'em!"

More shots rang out from the Confederate line and blue blood fell upon the ground. Some of the rebels thought it was an opportunity to move forward and did without orders. They ran toward the Union line, jumping over the fence; others shot dead before reaching the fence. The small assault was quickly repelled. The few that made it to the Union line and lived fell back to their own line. Some of the rebels were shot in the back while attempting to flee to their original lines.

Lining his men up, Joshua fired three volleys into the Union…the orders came to fall back once again. He was flabbergasted at the notion to retreat. He knew the Union

Chapter Eight

line had been reinforced but knew with one great push with the whole division they could overtake the enemy.

For the second time they fell back to regroup and reload. Some fell to the ground, others stood or knelt. Joshua looked at his men, their numbers dwindling down in vast numbers. He took another drink of water in an attempt to refresh his throat from yelling and cool his mind. It didn't work very well.

"Sir, why don't we just take em?"

"Yeah, we could whoop em if we was allowed to advance and charge at em!"

"Yeah!"

The men began to shout and yell their complaints. Joshua hushed them and told them that even he had to follow orders, no matter how ludicrous they were. While he was explaining to his men what was to happen, a captain to Colonel Fry came down the line to give new orders.

"Lieutenant Anderson!"

"Yes, sir."

" We have orders coming down from General Archer. He has informed the division to hit them again, get their line moving and charge forward. Attempt to flank the enemy on their left. He seems to think they are weakest on that point."

"Yes, sir. We are to take the enemy line, understood!"

"Very good, God go with you."

"And you, sir."

The men of his company were hot, weary and almost at the point of being misguided within their souls. The hot July heat was getting to them along with the heat of the raging battle. The wool uniforms and pants clung to their sweaty bodies, not allowing the skin to breathe. The sweat poured from their heads, streaming down their faces and falling upon the necks. Heavy breathing and sloshing of canteens were heard all about the line.

The platoon was given the order by company commander to move the battle line forward once again. They fell in line but this was preceded by a large cannonade fire. Heth's fifteen guns had really begun to open up on the enemy.

"Forward march!" yelled Joshua, his voice becoming increasingly strained and hoarse.

The men lurched forward, walking up the crest of the hilly countryside. The plush green field was turning into a field of death. The grass was covered by red blood and gopher holes were filled with puddles of mud, water and blood. Detached limbs were strewn on the field. Men were forced to step on or over the dead and dying. All eyes were focused on the Union line, focused on the objective.

They continued to walk in the shin-high grass. Feet ached and felt like plows arduously tilling the field. Calloused minds and calloused feet united forward in thrusts of motion teeming them toward a hail of lead looking for a home in which to reside.

The men moved a bit farther up into the firing of the Union position. A cannon ball fell to the right of Joshua and caused a bit of grass and earth to rain down on him. All went silent as he fell to the ground. His body fell and hit the grass beneath him. Not a sound could be heard in his ears.

He felt his body and noticed all was where it should be. Why couldn't he hear? What had happened? Sound was lost and he looked around in a daze. His men, as well as many others, were moving forward. Bodies fell to the ground, hoards of men looked to be screaming. He could feel a cannon fire from off in the distance and watched it hit a group of men. Limbs and torsos went flying through the air. Joshua slowly lifted himself from the ground. His hearing began to return. He could mostly hear the sound of his own breathing.

He stood completely and ran to rejoin his platoon. He put his sword back into its scabbard and withdrew his fire shot

Chapter Eight

revolver. He put extra shells into his other hand to make sure they were there quickly when he needed to reload. Joshua began shouting, trying to hear over his own voice. His breathing quickened and then all sound began to be restored. The battle revived itself in his eardrums. He continued to bark out orders to his men.

The regiment fired three volleys into the bluebellies, then began to move slightly forward. They reloaded while walking toward the fence row of blue men. A hot moving fire continued from the enemy. Joshua noticed it had died down a bit. He marched his men forward, close enough to hear the Union commanders yelling as well.

Joshua gave the command to halt and then aim and fire. The muzzles of the platoon poured out their death as they were so close that it went through the wooden fence and hit their targets. He yelled out the order to reload and fix bayonets and the men did as commanded.

They reloaded in order to have one last volley of musket fire. Metal clanked on metal as shaking hands put on the cold steel of death at the end of their muskets. The order came down the line, fire and charge. They marched forward just a little more and gave the command to fire upon the enemy.

The Union fell in great number as the Confederate soldiers put their bullets into them. One by one the enemy fell. Then came that awful high pitched yell that many Union men would hear in their sleep for the rest of their lives. The Rebel yell!

"Forward men. Charge the enemy line. Make 'em run boys!" screamed Joshua.

The platoon moved quickly forward and ran toward the fence line of blue soldiers. They yelled and belched out their wail at the top of their lungs. The Union didn't turn and run though, they held fast, digging their heels in, firing into the Confederate soldiers. The platoon and Joshua reached the fence row and leaped over the fence.

Bayonets jabbed into men after being thrust through the air. Men bellowed out in pain and slumped to the ground. Rifles, muskets and anything they had in their hand went swinging in the air. Jaws crunched and bones split as bayonets and rifles met their targets. It was now hand to hand as Joshua's men leaped over the fence.

Joshua fired his pistol at the enemy, the bullets plowing through their bodies. As he stopped moving forward to reload, a Calvary man ran toward Joshua sword in hand. Joshua looked up and then back down repeatedly as he began to fumble with the bullets in the attempt to reload. The man closed in on him and sent his saber flying through the air to crash down on Joshua's head.

Joshua flinched, for he knew the end had come, but then a shot to his left rang out. The Union man stumbled and fell to the ground in front of him. Looking to his left he saw Private Walker lowering his rifle and smiling. Joshua nodded at him, but at that moment a blue belly came quickly and stabbed Walker in the back with his bayonet. Joshua aimed at the man and fired his pistol. The bullet went streaming through the air and hit the man in the head. With his skull broken in pieces the man fell to the ground. Joshua ran to the private.

"Private! Private!" he shouted.

"Sir..." wincing in pain the private couldn't speak.

"Private don't talk. But look, you have those bluebellies on the run!"

Walker looked up and saw the Union Calvary running away trying to reform at a different location.

"Private, you have certainly restored your family!"

Walker couldn't speak. A tear formed in his eyes and he began to cough, his head convulsing. Blood poured from his mouth. Then his eyes glazed and the heavy breathing stopped. He was at peace. Joshua looked at him one time more before moving on ahead with his troops.

Chapter Eight

He ran forward and tried to find his platoon. There was mass confusion as he ran. Some stragglers of the Union Army lagged behind and were captured. Most of the men ran forward and continued to push the advance. Joshua stopped to look around attempting to find a familiar face. He began to gain his bearing and found his platoon. They had stopped to rest a bit before pushing on and were lingering beneath a tall oak tree. No orders were given and it was not quite clear what they were to do.

Small fights were breaking out and the fighting was confused. Battle lines were not drawn and blue and gray uniforms began to mix together. From amidst the fray came Captain Robinson.

"Fall back! Fall back! We must reform on that ridge over there!" he yelled while pointing his finger at the hill they had just come from.

"Sir, why?" Joshua asked.

"They have infantry support. Orders are to fall back and regroup."

"Yes, sir."

"Quickly men, get out of this railroad cut," yelled Robinson.

Gathering his platoon, they moved out with extreme haste. They double timed toward their position, where the division was forming. He looked back for just a moment as they ran to reform on a small knoll. He could see a line of blue soldiers marching down the road toward them. Some Confederates fell at the railroad cut, having to give over their weapons.

The captain gave the order to move into the woods and left of their position.

"If we move over to those woods we will have cover and be able to attack the Union line from a better angle," yelled Captain Robinson.

"Sir, those woods seem to be very dense and could prove to trap us in."

"I assure you, I have scouted it out and it will prove to be a better position. Let's move quickly the Union line is advancing. They seem to be relieving the calvary," said Robinson.

"Yes, sir. I will move my platoon. Move to the right men. Get into the woods and find cover. We will slowly advance on the enemy position from there. Fire then reload from cover. Alright, let's move boys, double time!" yelled Joshua.

He moved his company into the woods south of the Chambersburg Pike. Stepping over fallen trees and stumps was slowing them down. Any kind of formation that they may have been in was now gone. The brush had been cut recently so that made the march a bit easier. They began to see the end of the woods facing Gettysburg. That is where they saw the blue line of soldiers.

Muskets came to life as each side fired at the other. Minie balls and stone bullets went flying through the air. A round hit the tree next to Joshua and sent shards of bark and rock soaring above him. He shielded his face as bits of shrapnel hit his arm. He winced in pain and shouted out to return fire.

"Fire at will boys!"

The company returned the Union fire and took cover behind the trees or rocks to reload. Looking out of the woods, Joshua saw a man atop a horse. A very elegant man. As shots rang out he watched the man fall from the horse and slump upon the ground. Joshua continued to fire his pistol at the enemy, even though his left arm had begun to ache tremendously.

He tore his jacket sleeve and noticed the shrapnel had slightly penetrated the skin. Joshua withdrew his knife and plucked out the bark and shredded lead. He wrapped the wound with a handkerchief from his pocket. Looking up, he

Chapter Eight

noticed the Union infantry attempting to move forward onto his position.

"Push em back boys! Hit em hard!"

The Confederate rifles came to life causing many of the enemy to fall. The Union slumped back to their position, men dragging others away from the field of battle.

"Move forward men!"

The men came from their places of cover and began to move forward into the Union line. The enemy opened up on Joshua's men and the death toll began to rise. Men fell in the brush piles and over fallen trees. They stumbled and fell over branches, nonetheless they pushed forward, advancing on the enemy's position.

"Take cover and return fire!"

The company fell behind whatever trees they could find to protect themselves from the Union guns. From these positions they aimed their muskets at the enemy, pulled the triggers; the flintlock fell down on the nipple causing the weapon to fire. They were able to reload from their cover causing the casualties to remain lower than the enemy.

Leaning out from behind his tree, Joshua was able to see the enemy very clearly. They adorned their black hats, information that might be key to the General. Out of the chaos came an alarming, startling tap on his shoulder.

"Lieutenant?"

Turning quickly, his pistol in hand, Joshua said, "Yes, sir?" It was Captain Robinson.

"We have orders for a full offensive upon the enemy."

"Sir? What have we been doing?"

"General Lee has given permission for us to attack, not play defense. Move your company forward with the rest of the regiment and overtake the Union line. I hear we got Ewell's whole corp now and Early's coming down on them from the North. We got em Lieutenant. Move out!"

"Yes, sir." Robinson left to move his way to others.

"Charge forward, men, forward! Take em out!"

The high pitched scream belched out and the rebels advanced. They ran headlong into the enemy, rifles high above their heads, swinging wildly. The black hats stuck to their lines, not moving.

The Union's right flank had begun to retreat causing those positioned in front of Joshua to also retreat. The enemy with the black hats had no other choice but to fall back. The Union ran towards the town with whoops and hollers crying out from the Rebels.

Chapter Nine

◆

Ephesians 6: 10,11

Finally, be strong in the Lord and in his mighty power. Put on the full armor of God so that you can take your stand against the devil's schemes.

July 1, 1863

The youth flashed in his mind. The boy had no facial hair, but long dark hair flowed from his head. His face screamed innocence caught by the ravages of war. A small breeze tussled his hair as a shot rang out in silence. The boy winced in pain and cried out. The fear of death flickered in his eyes as he slowly fell to the ground. Still. Lifeless. Eyes wide open to the sky above him, he looked as he was praying. James looked down at his hand. The revolver's smoking barrel was hot and fiery red. There was blood on the trigger. There was blood everywhere. The face of the boy stared at him. Eyes fixed upon him in a gaze they locked eyes. Why? Why? He heard the voice as everything turned to red. Everywhere he looked he saw red.

"Spalding!"

James awoke from the dream sequence, the silent memories running through his mind came to an end. Startled by the voice, he was breathing heavy as if he had sprinted a mile. His breathing began to slow as his senses began to quicken.

"Captain," General Buford's voice was gruff and firm.

"Yes, sir", replied Jim focusing on the man behind the voice.

"For God's sake, I cannot afford to lose you. You are part of my staff. Get back to the seminary."

"Sir I respectfully ask to stay. We need every man on this line. The way those rebs keep coming at us…"

"I lose you, I lose one of my engineers. I can't do this."

Captain Spalding stared at him blankly.

General Buford growled, "Give me your maps then. Can't afford to keep them here."

Trotting over to his horse, James pulled the sweating leather saddle bag off and handed it to the general.

"Very well." Buford walked hastily toward his horse, mounted and rode off without saying anything else.

James returned to the line and reloaded his pistol, turning to the man next to him to ask a question but stopped. The body was slumped over the second rail of the fence, his eyes glossy and lifeless. He stared into the eyes.

"Here they come!"

Locking the cylinder of his revolver into place, James synced the barrel with the bullets. The firearm felt heavy in his hands, the grip seemed slick in his palm. He wiped his hands on his trouser hoping the sweat would subside for a moment. Nervousness swelled within his stomach, as he attempted to calm the visceral reaction from the top of his throat.

"Hold your fire until they get closer men!" yelled a company commander.

It felt as though there was a struggle within his ears, whether he heard the grassy footsteps of the enemy making

Chapter Nine

their way up the slope toward their line, the roaring cannons firing off near him or perhaps his own heart was beating so fiercely his throat pulsated. There were no drums or fife belting out a chorus to inspire…

The streets were filled with blue uniforms in lines and the brass beamed while the drums rattled. Cobblestone roads sang to the beat of the percussion while white hankies were waved through the air like miniature flags of joy and sorrow. The smiles of men rang out from toothy grins and pride…

"How stupid we were."

"What sir?"

"Oh, nothing."

"Take aim boys!"

James lifted his pistol, the weight was almost too much, his arm felt like a person sat upon it. He pulled the trigger for a second, minute, it felt like a year as the sight on the other end was a man whom he did not know, and did not hate. The trigger struck the firing pin sparking the black powder and pushing the bullet from the barrel. Kicking back in his hands, it shocked him at the ease in which a human being just died.

"Fire at will lads," yelled Gamble. "We'll have the day that is for sure. I want a cloud of fire around those rebs."

His pistol continued to fire and with each shot it became easier to draw down on a person pick his target and squeeze. With the gun clicking, he lowered the instrument and opened the barrel exposing the spent shells, lifting it in the air the cartridges streamed through the air and clinked on the sod below him. Jamming six more shots into the barrel, he was once more able to aim his pistol down on the advancing enemy.

"They want a fight, and that's what they are getting laddies. We are going to give it to them hot and we're going to give it to them heavy," Gamble attempted to yell above the atrocious din. "Don't let them flank you boys. Watch the flank, they're attempting to move to the left, cut 'em off. Pour into them there boys!"

The commanders responded, shifting fire to the left of their position. The rebels fell back into their original positions.

The rebels inched their way closer, a volley was sent into their lines, but a section of the Confederates charged at James' position. A rebel came to him, but his pistol clicked and didn't fire. The man was atop of him, pushing the rifle into his throat cutting off the air supply that allowed life. His eyes grew wide as the rifle crushed his wind pipe his final breaths inching from him, the world began to become fuzzy and the sun above his head dilated his pupils. The only thing to be seen was a bright light...

Chapter Ten

◆

Micah 5:2

But you, Bethlehem Ephrathah,though you are small among the clans of Judah, out of you will come for me one who will be ruler over Israel, whose origins are from of old, from ancient times.

July 1, 1863

"*I* was told no action," belted out Heth. "This is not what was to happen. I was told only militia!"
"Sir.."
"I do not wish to hear excuses!" Heth lifted his field glasses to his face. "Someone put more fire on that ridge there. Where is the artillery?"
"Sir, the guns are deploying now," his aide replied.
A rider approached the general waving his hat. It was a major from Lee's camp. "Sir, General Lee wishes for you to return to the rear in order to give a report of what is happening."
"Lead the way," replied Heth. "Major, make sure there is fire on that ridge."
"Yes, sir."

****

Buford peered out onto the battlefield from the cupola. He stared through his glasses, the battle raged in front of his eyes. Cannon balls screamed through the air causing bright flashes to streak across the late morning horizon. The smoke from muskets and rifles caused a fog to settle on each battle line. The smell of gun powder filled the nostrils of each man. Wagons exploded, ground shook, men soaring through the air, horses falling.

His stomach was nauseated, a galvanic feeling that the line wouldn't hold. Buford stood atop of the cupola, eyes cemented to his looking glasses, watching the gray line advance on his boys. "Get word down to Gamble it looks as if they might try and flank again."

He fixed his gaze to the southwest, then southeast. Nothing. Reynolds was not here yet. It made him more nervous, more anxious. He knew the Rebels would come back with the whole division and over run them. It was just a matter of time, just a fact that Buford had to live with.

He galloped toward battle, his aide trying to keep up. He pulled the reins and entered through a gap in the fence. The rebels were falling back, but would soon return with more men. Buford knew the line was getting tired. The heat and humidity was horrendous, sweat streamed down his back. He hopped off his horse and strode over to Colonel Gamble who was blowing his nose, obviously not doing well with all the fields and trees.

"General, they'll be back any minute," said Gamble.

"I know Colonel, I know. I just wanted to see how things are going."

"Oh sir, they came up close but we handled them. We gave them a chance to surrender. Some did. Put them in the rear. Let the Provost Marshal handle them."

"Good. How is the line?"

Chapter Ten

"Fine, sir. Just fine. We're getting a little tired. This heat is terrible. I worry the line won't hold for too much longer though sir." Gamble sneezed.

Buford stood there for a moment surveying the damage that his brigades had sustained. The dirty faces stared at him and he stared in disbelief, silently allowing his thoughts to stray away. The general said nothing to Gamble allowing the eye contact and salutes to vociferate their words.

Climbing the steps once again, he returned to the top of the cupola. He stared out at the line and saw some of the men falling back. Part of the line was holding well, but it would not take long to break. He considered giving the order to retreat. His eyes scrunched together watching the lines begin to fold. Both Devin's and Gamble's brigades began to fall backwards toward the ridge the seminary was built upon. Buford almost gave that command for a full out retreat, but turned and looked to the south. Reynolds.

The elegant horseman bounded toward the seminary and found Buford standing atop the church.

"John?" shouted Reynolds.

"We need support, sir, and fast."

"Well, we are here."

"I'm coming down, sir."

Buford's steps were light yet burdened. Each foot reached in front of each other seemingly laden with mirth yet with a sapience of dread. From within the dark seminary emerged General Buford, squinting his eyes until the retinas became accustomed to the bright light emitting from the welkin.

"Quite a feat you have done here, John," said Reynolds looking down at Buford from atop his horse.

"Give credit to my men, sir."

"Well, do you know what we are facing in front of us?"

"Yes, sir. Right now Heth is attacking, Early's corp is coming up fast, behind that is Longstreet. From the north is General Ewell's corp."

"With what is happening now, we have two more corps coming up. I feel that we will be alright. General Sickles and Doubleday are behind me, Hancock after that."

"Hopefully…"

"Yes. Thank your men for me. This was quite a stand you made. Much applause and appreciation. You may begin to pull your troops off the line. We will attack from here."

"Yes, sir."

Buford gave the command to Gamble to start pulling the troops off the line and then rode back to Reynolds. General Reynolds was giving command to his aides, who quickly scurried off.

"General Reynolds. How is that little lady of yours?"

"She is sick from worry. I still have not come up with a way to tell my family. I guess I'll figure it out somehow."

"You are very fond of her aren't you?"

"She is the love of my life, John. Without her, I am lost. I can't quite figure out how I have managed so far."

"I have heard from many people that she feels the exact same way."

"With luck we can see all of our loved ones again."

Buford gave command to his aide. He turned in his saddle and looked at Reynolds. A shot rang out from the woods. A shot of which amalgamated with all the other shots. It was rivulet with all the other grains of destruction flying about. Reynolds stood straight up in the saddle slumping forward, his head landing on the mane of his horse before his body rolled off and hewed to the hot bloody ground below him.

Buford commanded Reynolds' body to be taken to the rear, the musket balls now streaming over his own head and nicking his tunic…

****

Chapter Ten

General Heth rode next to General Lee, listening avidly to the gentle voice disciplining him for the action. "With the forces in the north coming down to meet us here, attack General Heth. Full out."

"Yes, sir," responded Heth.

Heth rose within the saddle and kicked the transport to full stride, the legs spraying the dirt high behind him, dust rising in the air. The delirium of his heart was heard in the thunderous steps of the horse the piquancy of its breath.

****

Meade rode past some caissons, trying to find his new headquarters in the dark. He had been in a terrible mood all day and now his head began to hurt. His son rode beside him always and he could hear him talking about the sword he had found.

"Took it off a dead reb soldier not too far back," he boasted. Meade paid no attention to him, he was tired and knew there was much more work to be done.

His mind hard at work, he wondered what kind of army he had left. There was a fight and he had received all the reports. Sickles and his men fell back again, he cursed the man in his mind. He had received a report from General Hancock that he had rallied the men from running and formed defensive positions south of town on a ridge near a cemetery. They had good ground, high ground, Hancock reported. Meade had hoped the ground was good enough for the army.

Meade had just taken over. He was not yet prepared to fight such a large scale engagement. He wanted to speak with his generals, get a feel about the people. He wanted to get the attitudes put aside and win this godforsaken mess that the war had turned into. A man pointed the way to his headquarters and he pulled into camp. He dismounted and the people that were arguing stopped and snapped to attention, though he paid no mind and opened the door.

He bellowed out for somebody to inform him about the situation. Hancock came over to him. "Sir, if you look at the maps, I'll show you what had happened and where we are currently positioned."

"Show me, Win," replied Meade. They walked over to the table where Buford had dropped the maps.

"Sir, this is where General Buford halted the enemy." Hancock said pointing to the area west of town. "Now we are here, on this ridge. We stretch from this cemetery down to this knoll," Hancock's finger moved along the map, "and we are positioned here on Culp's hill which hooks around to here."

"Well this had better be good. I most assuredly do not want to fight right now, but it looks as though we have no choice."

"Well, Sir, you shall be glad we stayed. I'm sure of it."

"I hope you are right. I hope you are."

****

"This is more than just militia sir," an aide stated.

"I can see that!" screamed General Archer. "I can see that it is dismounted cavalry." General Pettigrew strode toward the general each other meeting eyes.

"It's a bit more than we thought, eh James."

Archer said nothing, only gave him a sullen look.

"I knew it, General I knew it," said Pettigrew.

"General that does not matter now. What matters now is only *how* we react."

They looked through their glasses just a moment longer. "That's it boys," yelled Archer. "I'm going up there."

"General that's dangerously close," belted out Pettigrew. But General Archer had already kicked his horse.

Chapter Ten

****

"John, where do you think you're goin?"

"I'm not gonna allow them rebs to tramp into my town," yelled Burns, pulling on his blue swallowtail coat. He grabbed his flintlock and powder horn, closing the door behind him.

He stepped haughtily down his road leading himself into a sequence of horror and death. Finding a wounded soldier he asked to use his rifle and picked it up setting his elder down. "Permission to join the fight? " he asked a major.

Major Chamberlin looked him over, up and down. "I suppose," he replied with one eyebrow lifted.

He marched on the outside of the formation, the battle within its adolescence. Each shot he fired brought back the ease of fighting and the horrors of death. Moving down the line meeting boys from the same home and from the Midwest before the line broke and a tumultuous frenzy occurred.

A sharp pain coursed through his arm, then leg while a burning sensation could be felt in his chest. He fell hard to the ground his arms not breaking his fall. He crawled… "I have to bury this," he thought of his ammunition… one arm in use dragged himself… the flare of light and the darkness…

****

"General Archer that's too far forward," yelled Pettigrew to himself, looking through his glasses. "Get back up! Get back up!"

****

"General Heth the men are pushing the enemy back sir, we have to get back to the rear sir. We are, in fact, in a very heated area."

"I need to see my boys, I need to…" another shot rang out that fused with all the other ones. Heth fell from his horse…blood from his head.

"General!!!"

****

"Who are you?" asked the confederate.

"I am a resident here. I was looking for help for my wife, she isn't well."

"Hmm." The man went away for a few moments conferring with another confederate. His boots thumped as he returned. "You know what the penalty is for being a civilian combatant?"

"I was just looking for…"

"It is death sir." John Burns could only stare at him.

****

"Lay him down here," said an orderly.

"General Heth is quite lucky," stated a surgeon directing it toward General Pettigrew.

"Is he well?" asked Pettigrew.

"He is unconscious, but will survive. He should have a nasty ache when he rises."

"Well, at least he is here. General Archer is … gone. Last saw him falling from his horse."

"Yes sir."

****

The fire crackled in the early morning hours, flames danced as they flickered through the air. Joshua and other officers were sitting around a thick stump next to the fire

Chapter Ten

where they played poker. There was conversation and laughter.

"Show us what you have, Bob." prompted Joshua.

"I have," Bob cleared his throat, "a pair of aces." The men moaned and most of them turned their cards over.

"Ahh..full house!" exclaimed Joshua. Bob shook his head and threw the cards down on the stump. The other officers laughed and patted Bob on the shoulders, joking and nudging him. Another lieutenant came over to the others and sat down a perplexed look on his face.

"What's the matter?" asked Joshua.

"Just got back from the hospital."

"Where is that?"

"In a barn off the road we came in on. Saw General Heth."

The men all started asking questions at once, clamoring to find out Heth's condition. "He was shot in the head and he's gonna make it just fine. He's unconscious. They stitched him up and set him aside."

"Sit down and join the game." Joshua said to the lieutenant. All eyes on him, he sat and the cards were dealt.

"What were we talking about?" asked Cooper.

"We was discussin' the way them bluebellies run again. They always running!" chortled Bob.

"Quite right you are. You see, they ain't fightin' for nothin'. We is fightin' for our freedom. A man fights differently when his own home has been invaded." said Cooper.

"Yes, but now we have invaded their home," said the lieutenant.

"Always negative with you John." said Joshua. "We are fightin' for our freedom. Freedom from taxation without representation. The control of government that sticks their head in our business. They make up new laws without any reason and we fightin' against it, just like with the Brits in the Revolution. Just like Bob fights with his wife." A chorus of laughter sang out.

"Now, you see here Mr. Anderson," Bob slurred, a bit tipsy. After a gentle reminder of Joshua's rank, "I'm sorry *Lieutenant* Anderson." Bob laughing said, "You see the reason my wife and I fight is cause she got no sense. She is always buttin in my ways. She don't know no better, she's a woman." Another chorus of laughter.

"Sir, I do believe that you are stepping into the fire, so to speak. I have met your wife. She is a lovely woman and I believe that you are full of the spirits!" said Joshua. "I think we should all toast to our women!"

"Look who's talkin' and toastin', the unmarried one! The bachelor's tellin us to toast our women!" hollered Bob slightly leaning to the left.

"The lieutenant is right. While we are at war, they are too. They put up with our absence and keep the home lights burning. We should honor them with our drink!"

As one, they raised their flasks to what the captain had said. "Here, here!" one chimed as they took a swig.

"Gentlemen, it is very late and tomorrow is a new day. I am going to retire. I will see you in the morning." said Joshua.

The men laughed at him and made comments about tucking him into bed. He drifted away from the laughter to a large tree where his knapsack dangled from a low hanging branch. Rolling out his blanket upon the ground he prayed himself to sleep.

****

"He is still out?" asked Buford.

"Yes, sir," replied Matt. "I am watching him though. Doctor said he could be out for a while but luckily his throat wasn't crushed."

Chapter Ten

"Very well," Buford left.

Matt stayed by James' side talking to him knowing that there would be no response. People asked why he was talking to him. "Just in case."

"I think you will be a great father... I'm glad we are brothers since we have always been friends... I will not say anything like the L word to you... Cannot wait to eat some of my wife's pie... I wonder what our wives are doing right now..."

Matt drifted into slumber in the field, the stars peeking from behind clouds periodically.

****

He crawled in the darkness of night, allowing his memory of the streets to guide his way. The dirt on the roads and fields made it increasingly difficult to keep the dressed wounds from getting sullied. Each push of the feet and pull of the arm increased the pain from intolerable to devastating wishing for relief or death. John Burns crawled to the safety of a basement, friends carrying him back to his home in town. "John!" cried his wife. "Fetch the doctor..." Flickering eyes and blackening lights engulfed his visions. "Oh John, you old man..."

Chapter Eleven

Judges 2:16

Nevertheless the LORD raised up judges, which delivered them out of the hand of those that spoiled them.

July 2, 1863

Joshua rolled over on his side, the blanket wet with sweat, his knee hitting a root causing a reaction which woke him from his light sleep. The sweat on his forehead dripped into his eye, stinging he wiped it with what was left of his sleeve. The sun was just beginning to bring forth its orange and yellow glaze as if the earth was the cake while the sun became the frosting. Anderson felt as though he was in the hot woodstove oven his mother and sister would cook upon.

Propping himself up, his back leaning against the tree where he had slept, he rested his elbows on his knees the palms of his hands cupping the cheeks upon his face he lingered in thought. Joshua's thoughts became of Alabama and his family. The letters men in his company received from their loved ones and the lack of his. It filled him with a solicitous feeling, one which made his eyes begin to tear.

Chapter Eleven

Shaking the feeling from his head he attempted to think of different times, a point in his mind that made him smile. Joshua thought of Katrina, the neighboring farmgirl who used to run around his house barefoot. She smiled with such intensity the upper lip would curl up and disappear from the rest of her mouth.

Footsteps behind him caused him to turn. "Nate."

"Josh."

"What are you up to this fine morning?"

"Just trying to avoid the heat but that's provin to be somethin' hard."

"I know it. I was just thinking about home."

"Well there sure is lots to think about. Sure do miss it."

"Yeah."

"You still ain't heard from them yet."

"No."

"I'm sure they're fine. You know how they are. Busy... bodies."

"They are not!" Joshua looked at Nate, who was silently chuckling to himself. "You think you're somethin' funny don't you?"

"Of course. You wanna go for a walk or somethin'?"

"Not really. Legs are tired. Aren't yours?"

"Not really. You gotta remember, I actually ride my horse. I'm lazy," Nate laughed.

They sat there, looking at the sun reminiscing about sunrises of past days and littered the tree with their bodies. The early morning quickly became full morning with the eastern sun warming their bodies and bringing a certain amount of a soporific sensation upon them. Their eyes drifted into the recesses of their brains lifting them to be home for a little while.

"I could eat," said Nate waking Joshua.

"Hum," responded Joshua.

"Come on wake up. We can go get something in our bellies."

"I'm comin."

He lifted himself to his elbows, looking at the eastern sun coming up over the horizon. The tops of houses and buildings shone the sunlight giving the homes a resilient look about them. Rolling over on his knees Joshua lifted himself up to the day ahead, they turned their heads as in the distance a cannon fired and muskets performed the symphony of destruction.

"Think we'll see somethin' today?" asked Nate.

"Don't rightly know," replied Josh.

"No matter what happens, I'm tired that's for sure."

"Yeah." They walked to a tent housing food.

The tent, filled with smoke and fires burning, produced a sound which caused stomachs to churn with excitement toward the prospect of food. Bacon sizzled in the pans while stacks of pancakes piled the plates awaiting eager hands to sequester them to the confines of their bodies. Nate and Joshua took their food, finding themselves a nice seat of sod and grass to sit on while eating in silence. The food was welcomed within their stomachs each man enjoying each other's company.

"What do ya see when you look at the enemy Nate?"

"Whatcha mean?"

"Do you feel weird, shootin at a man you don't even know?"

"No."

"Why?"

"Never thought about it really. I guess I never put much thought into things like that."

Joshua gave him a look to signify his disbelief.

"Look. When someone starts thinkin' too much they get to be hurtin' too much. If I started thinking about all the men

Chapter Eleven

that have shot at me or that I have shot, I would end up not shootin' back and then where'd I be? I'd be dead."

"Or the most alive you've ever felt."

"I don't follow you Josh."

"I don't know, just talkin'. You ever feel like you're committin' some kind of crime though, not against country, but against men?"

"I think that if we start thinkin' that way we are useless again. Josh we ain't done nothin' back home but plow fields. Here we mean somethin'."

"At what cost though Nate? I'm troubled by what happened yesterday."

"What happened that was any different than all the other engagements we were in."

"Walker died."

"He was a good man for sure, but we all seen people die. Every time we step out on those long bloody fields someone dies and it's just a matter of time afore we do. Are you afraid of death then? Is that it?" asked Nate.

"No," replied Joshua. "I just, I guess maybe I'm just tired."

"Ok. We will be resting today anyway, so just nap all day."

"How can I, hearing those cannons in the distance."

Nate looked toward the sounds then back to his friend. "Heard a lot of men wonder where God is in all this destruction and all this hurt."

"God? God is where He has always been." Joshua stared with question filled eyes. "He hasn't stopped being God, we've just stopped being humans."

Chapter Twelve

◆

Luke 9:24

For whosoever will save his life shall lose it: but whosoever will lose his life for my sake, the same shall save it.

July 2, 1863

*H*e bolted straight up, breathing heavily, sweat pouring from his body and running down his forehead. For a moment he sat there, trying to catch his breath. He looked around the dimly lit tent, trying to get his eyes to focus. Spinning his legs around, he let his feet rest on the ground, but didn't attempt to move from his cot. James put his right hand to his forehead, wiping away the sweat then just rubbing his temples with his thumb and middle finger. His left arm rested on his thigh, his hand gripping his knee.

Again the nightmare. The same recurring nightmare. He saw the young boy, blood everywhere. His breathing slowed and he now sat with both arms on his legs, slightly shaking his head to get the vision out. Fully awake, having slept what seemed like only minutes, James pulled his pocketwatch out from his pants. Five in the morning, he squinted to see the dial as he wound the stem for the day. He slipped his pants

Chapter Twelve

on, slowly one leg then the other. Standing up, he pulled up his pants and slid his suspenders over his broad shoulders. James sat again and pulled his cavalry boots on, stomping each foot into the stiff leather. Standing up, he took in a deep breath, trying to shake the remnants of the visions, telling himself it was just a nightmare. Remembering the nightmare had actually happened made him feel ill.

He put on his heavy, sweat stained tunic, he buttoned the brass buttons. "It's war. Innocence is gone," he told himself aloud. It didn't comfort him; it only made him feel more nauseous. He couldn't figure out what was bothering him, many soldiers died yesterday, why was this torturing him? He knew that there were kids in the Confederate Army, kids as young as twelve. Adorning his hat, he stepped outside his tent.

James looked over the vast ocean of campfires, noticing more troops had poured in through the short night while he slept. The sun was not fully awake, as the rays were just beginning to poke through the darkness, light coming much earlier this far east. Even in the semi-darkness, he could imagine the rolling hills of the countryside, reminding him of home. The hills of Gettysburg were similar to home, there was a familiar sense about it. After all, Pennsylvania did border New York.

The atmosphere felt very much alike in this small town to the one he knew back home. All small towns in the north had that feel, James had found out by riding through much of the land. No matter what small village he rode into, he felt at home. It was knowledge that everyone knew everyone. Each man or woman could walk down the walkways and cobblestone streets and tip their hats to one another. They would step into a shop and know the owner by name and the owner knew their name, and the names of all the family. He adored that feeling of love and kinship in a village. Having been to Washington, he knew he didn't like the hustle and bustle of the city. People walked by each other and didn't even say hello.

Here in this town, he felt at home. He didn't know any of the people, any of their names or problems, other than the big one on the outskirts of town. Still he felt a level of comfort being here, a sense that he recognized. James drew in another deep breath of country air, but it was filled with the acrid scent of campfire smoke and humidity. Adding to these were the odoriferous bodies still lying on the battlefield, unable to be retrieved or buried. That made James flash back to yesterday. He quickly shook the memory from his head.

Walking out to a clearing near the road, he moved away from the men lying in the field. Leaning up against a tree, he spoke to some of the men marching, but most either didn't see him because of the pale light or the increasing cloud cover. Lightning lit up the distant sky. Heat. Because of the light he couldn't see at all, but he could hear the sounds of war. The sounds were spectacular. The soldiers walking by him, their boots hitting the dirt and gravel of the road, crunched and ground and scuffed. The tinny clink of metal striking against each other. Leather belts creaked adding to the creaks of saddle and straps being moved or readjusted. Wagons noisily passed by, wooden wheels rolling over ruts and rocks causing it to jump up and down, bouncing whatever lay under the tarps. Horses walked past, their hooves pounding the dirt, snorting and shaking their large heads in the morning air as they not only carried riders, but pulled caissons of ammunition and cannons of destruction.

James lived off a river and at night he could sit on his porch in town and listen to the river sounds. It would make that noise, almost like the noise of the wind racing through tree leaves. The sounds of running water, hitting and licking the rocks, flowing quickly down the bed. The marching army reminded him of the river. The water kept coming and

Chapter Twelve

coming, so did the men and wagons. The voices in the night rang out like the water battering the side of a large rock.

They were talking softly to themselves, mostly about home, food and of course women. Some men would walk close enough to James to see him, ask him what outfit he was with, and kept on moving, wanting to get to wherever they were heading. He reached in his pocket and pulled out a cigar, lit it and puffed on the sweet invigorating taste. The burning end could be seen in the semi-darkness as it glowed when he inhaled. He exhaled and released a cloud of smoke into the inky morning atmosphere. His nerves were beginning to settle and he could now focus on the day.

James left the river of wagons and men and went back to his saddle bags. He opened his leather case, the material creaking as it rubbed against the back. Lifting his sword and pistol belt from the ground, he wrapped it around his waist. He took out his box of cigars from his bags, opened the top and took out a handful. After putting these in his jacket pocket, he closed the lid and put the box back in the container. Shutting the lid, he snapped open his black leather holster and pulled his 1860 Colt from its resting place. He pressed down on the cylinder release and the barrel and chambers popped down. Checking to see if it were fully loaded, he found that in the confusion of yesterday he had forgotten to do so and began the task. Taking out the five empty cartridges, he put in five new brass rounds. He slammed the revolver shut and put in into his holster and made sure his belt was fully loaded with ammunition as well.

James picked up the brush from a wooden bucket and began to stroke the horse's dark brown hair. "Well, my dear Tulip, I do hope you are rested. We shall be riding today and riding hard, I am sure." James continued to brush as he talked, the horse turning her neck and snorting through her nose as if agreeing this time. "You have truly proven yourself on the battlefield. I feel I can trust you more that my pistol." The horse again turned her head to him, this time to nibble gently on his arm. "My dear, I do believe we should keep this professional," chuckled Jim.

When he had finished brushing the noble beast, James threw a blanket on her back and then tossed the saddle over the blanket. He bent grabbing the straps at her underbelly and adjusted the leather listening to them creak and moan as he tightened them. Placing the bit in her mouth, he cinched the halter tight, gathered the reins in his hands and hoisted himself up on the horse. "Alright, my Tulip, take me to Gamble," he said spurring her gently and pulled left on the reins.

James rode out to the road he had stood beside earlier and headed north. He was among the hoards of men and wagon trains as he traveled a large burly man rode his horse up next to him.

"Who ya with?" asked the gruff man.

"U.S. Calvary."

"Ah, Buford's boys?"

"That is correct uh...Major," James said after he looked at the man's shoulder insignia.

"It's been circulating around about you boys holdin' your own. Is that true?"

"We did. Yes we held long enough for the infantry to come up."

"Phewee. That's amazin'. May I shake your hand?"

The two men shook hands and the major stated he had to return to his men and left. James didn't get his name but was embarrassed by his praises. Turning into Gamble's camp, he saw the man outside his tent, as always, blowing his nose.

James dismounted and strode over to the colonel, after exchanging salutes they sat down together. Gamble continued to eat. He drank his coffee while offering some to James. He accepted and sat down across the small fire the two men looking at each other.

Chapter Twelve

"Well, the General is a-might pleased with you boys," said Gamble between bites. "He said he knew why he had picked his men." Gamble went on praising and glorifying the brigades.

"Sir."

"Well, the general is gone to receive orders from headquarters. He'll be back soon with Devin. I guess we're to wait until then. Last I heard, we'll be protecting supply trains to and from the lines, but that you already know."

"Yes, sir." The two men continued to converse for a short while.

"Tell me, what do you think of all this? I'm a career man. I....I don't know what to make of it all. You're a Godly man, tell me."

"Well, sir," James spoke slowly, not really sure what to say. "At college we learned history. Sir...many nations have fought against themselves for many different reasons, but the ultimate outcome is the same, leadership. One person wants control of the land, the people. This is different....our civil war. We are not fighting for maintaining of our government, if we lost we would still have a president on Washington. The enemy, they fight for what they call freedom. They feel oppressed by our federal government and I guess I can see their point," James paused taking a sip of coffee, while Gamble listened attentively.

"Sir...this is a strange concept. I don't think many have ever stopped to think that we are fighting for two very big things. We first started this war; to preserve the Union. Sure the topic of slavery was hot and boiling the entire time. President Buchanan did nothing to prevent this from happening. But, after Antietam, with the President's Emancipation Proclamation, it became different. Yes, we still wish to hold this great nation together. Without us unified we would be subject to many invaders. Now...we fight for men, for oppressed men. This is something that I never learned about at school. No history book contained it, no sheet of paper described it. We are liberators sir. Men yoked together to set others free. We are not looking to establish a new government or to claim a throne. We are looking at giving men under God an opportunity that God has given us.

"Sir, God has given this country a great number of freedoms. Life, liberty and the pursuit of happiness. We created this nation under the eyes of God that all men are created equal and all men under God are free. We are free to choose God, speech and land. We can live where we want, eat what we want. This is truly the land of the free. God has ordained his conflict and God has ordained us to free his people, our people."

Gamble nodded his head up and down and let the words absorb into his brain. "Well put Captain," he finally said. "The truth is I have had trouble with commanding my boys to fire at them at times. They are still Americans whether they admit it or not. I have been troubled giving orders to kill my countrymen, my fellow citizens...my brothers. You see, all that we fight for is well and good. It is just and noble but in the end we are fighting family. I understand their cause, I really do. I understand our cause and our objective. I agree with you fully, Captain, but I feel alarmed that we are killing each other with such ease. I guess when the bullets and cannons begin to fire all our sense of decency and fair play goes away. But when you stop and think.....it bothers me. I wonder how all of this began. Yes, I know the firing on Fort Sumter and all that but...how does a brother kill a brother?"

"The Bible talks about this candidly, sir. Cain and Able. Joseph and his brothers. Jacob and Esau. I guess I wonder too, sir. The Bible speaks that it happens but never explains the human mind."

"That's what troubles me. That's what causes me to flinch when I give the command to attack." Gamble said rubbing the bridge of his nose with his thumb and index

Chapter Twelve

finger. Hearing approaching horses, the two men turned to see General Buford and Colonel Devin returning from headquarters. They rose to greet them as they dismounted.

"Gentlemen," said Buford, nodding his head in acknowledgment of their presence. "We have a long day ahead of us. Meade is very leery of the fact that Stuart is out there. We are to move out to Westminster, in Maryland. There we will be re-outfitted and protecting the supply trains that load and unload there. With the way Stuart has run around our army a few times, literally, Meade believes that our supplies need escorts. I will pass down orders to the both of you Colonel, you hand them out at your discretion."

The sun was just peaking and casting its rays down on the earth, raising the temperature of the land. James had left Gamble and slid his back down a tree, resting under the tall pine. As he sat there, his mind began to wander. The constant hoards of men made him flash to scenes of the day before. His eyes closed and his mind opened the floodgate of images permanently burned into his memory banks.

The blasts of muskets, the rising cloud of gun smoke, the cries of the wounded and the sight of blood on gorgeous green grass. The young boy. Bayonets being thrust through the air, butts of rifles swinging about. Bones crunching, teeth chattering, not from cold but from blows to the body and the sound of flesh being torn.

His eyes burst open, rose from the ground, mounted and kicked his horse to a trot. He left the pine tree and tried to get away from his memories. They followed him though, no matter how fast his horse would run. Finally he slowed her and made it back to the camp where his company was waiting. Dismounting, he found an empty place in the shade and sat. His mind turned now to his new child, his tiny little daughter.

He wanted to see her, wishing that the war had not been in the way of him doing that. James tried to place the child

Upon The Eastern Sun

in his mind, attempting to imagine what she looked like by the letter his wife had written. The eyes and nose and the tiny little hands. James' brother-in-law had a child not too long before the war broke out. His mind took him to that winter day of 1861, the day his brother handed the small package into his arms.

The fireplace was crackling and the baby was cooing. Matt was walking around with a cigar in his mouth, as the proud new father that he was. James was sitting on an old rocker next to the fire, watching his sister-in-law talk to his wife. Matt had walked over and handed the tiny newborn into his arms. Sitting there, he rocked the sleeping baby looking at his tiny little hands. Created from God and quite beautiful, the greatest of all comes in such a small package, he had thought.

A cannon shell burst in the distance and brought James back to the present. He lifted himself from the ground and brushed the dirt from his pants bending over to fix the hem, a deafening crack above him struck the tree spraying bark and wood chips over his entire body. He looked to the west of him and noticed smoke from the tree line and more sporadic musket fire spewing their balls. Dirt flew up in front of him and someone yelled, "Mount up, sniper fire!"

Rushing to his horse, he screamed at Matt to mount his mare. Matt threw his leg up over the hind end of the horse turning her with the reins to look back at James. A splatter of red came from Matt's chest flying through the air, sprinkling down to the tall grass below them. Falling, James reached him to help his fall from the mount.

"Matt!" He couldn't reply just look at him in disbelief. The horses ran with the rest of the tattered division leaving Matt and James in the midst of the sniper fire. "I have you," he yelled.

The leather harness on Matt's back made for handles as James dragged his brother-in-law to the rocks at the bottom

Chapter Twelve

of a hill. The sniper fire continued ricocheting off the rocks, pushing shards of stone into the faces of the two men. Hiding, James looked at Matt's wounds. Opening his tunic the white shirt underneath was saturated with red, the wound gaping with tissue and dirt lying on the top of the skin.

"Captain!" yelled a man scaring James.

Turning quickly, he heard an accent to the voice, his eyes large opened to the daylight. "Sergeant where did you come from?"

"Horse ran off. It was nicked by a sniper I think."

"Help me get Matt to a hospital."

The sergeant looked at the man, his eyes focusing on the wound. He lifted his head to look at James. "Uh sir…"

"Just help me please!" he pleaded.

"Yes, sir."

"Thank you."

The streams of sniper fire seemed to subside, so the two men picked up Matt, James putting his arms under Matt's armpits and lifting him down from the rocks. James walked backwards for a time, before stopping to rest. He gently set the head of his brother-in-law down on the ground.

"Captain, you're the General's engineer right?"

"Yes, uh sorry I do not know your name."

"Name is Bill Roberts."

"Oh. Yes, I am one of General Buford's engineers," replied James looking down at the hurting man. "We need to get moving again."

"Yes, sir." The two men picked Matt off of the ground once again, struggling to carry him to a hospital. "By the way sir, you never told me your name. You know this is a big outfit."

"Sorry. It's James Spalding."

"Captain Spalding," the man acknowledged with a quick nod of his head.

Blue uniforms became more of a commonality than a phenomenon. A barn with tents around the outskirts and canvas awnings covering some of the wounded stood before them. Flies swarmed around the wounds while hands waved them away. Screaming men engulfed their ears. "Set him down. I will get a doctor," said James.

Entering the barn, James heard men cursing and saw local women's aprons covered with blood. The doctor's arms were cutting with swift movements to not prolong the pain. He turned from the scene and threw up, wiping his mouth before entering again. "I need a doctor outside." No one returned his call or even turned to look. "I said I need a doctor outside!" he yelled this time.

A blood covered surgeon approached him. "Captain, everyone here needs a doctor. You can wait."

James finally noticed the blood on his tunic. "Not for me sir," he said, his eyes misting. "For my brother-in-law."

"Lead the way, Captain." The surgeon followed him through the maze of bodies watching each man lying upon the ground stiffened by fear and shock. One man spoke to himself while rocking back and forth. His eyes wide repeating the words, "Life is just windows, death a door."

As the surgeon knelt to look at Matt he moved the tunic aside and saw the wound. "He was dead shortly after the round hit him. There is nothing I can do."

"That is a lie! He can be saved!" screamed James.

"I am truly sorry captain." James pulled his pistol from its leather resting place. The doctor backed away slowly his arms outwards palms facing the weapon. "Captain... I am truly sorry that your brother-in-law is dead. But look around you. There are other brothers of yours I can save. Please let me do my work."

James scanned the bodies all now staring at him. Staring back at the doctor he began to pull the trigger...

Chapter Thirteen

◆

Daniel 6:21

Daniel answered, "O king, live forever!"

July 2, 1863

The coals of the fire smoldered, a light smoke drifting from the red glow. Distant musket fire from some probing pickets reverberated through the early morning air. The smells of war were inhaled by the unconscious man; fires of camp and cannons, make shift bathrooms in the woods, decaying flesh of the dead on the battlefield. A small downwind breeze blew the scents into his nostrils. The atrocious smells caused him to flutter to consciousness.

General Heth attempted to lift his head from his cot, but failed. His squinted eyes stared at the top of his tent, beginning to focus a bit. He lifted his hand to his head and felt a bandage tightly wound around his scalp. With each beat of his heart the pain throbbed through his head and coursed through his body. Heth made another attempt at sitting and with much agitation he had his feet planted on the ground.

The tent began to spin as he tried to stand. He fell backward, lying back down on his bed. Trying to call out to his aide, no sound would come. His breathing was getting heavier, causing his heart to beat faster, the pain intensified in his head. Finally enough strength came from his chest to call for his aide. The young man came running into Heth's tent, eyes half closed from sleep.

"Help me get ready for the day, Captain."

"Sir, I believe General Lee wants you to rest."

"Hogwash. I need to attend the meeting this morning," Heth said, breathing heavy, his eyes swimming. "I am assuming there are meetings, correct?"

"Yes, sir."

"Fine. Please help me steady myself."

The captain assisted the general in putting his jacket on and buttoning the tunic. Every motion seemed to be in slow motion and caused heavy breathing and a throbbing head.

"Sir, perhaps you shouldn't wear the hat with your wound."

"I think you are correct. I do believe that this hat saved my life, Captain, with the stuffed sheets."

"Sir, I would have to agree with you. Praise be the Lord for that oversized hat of yours."

"Thank you, Captain. Could you get my mount ready please?"

"Sir? Do you think it best to be riding in your condition?"

"I shall be fine. The dizziness comes and goes," lied Heth.

"Very well, sir. I will attend to it at once." The captain left the tent, rushing through the flaps, causing a burst of light, then dimness.

The general flopped himself down onto his wooden folding chair, causing it to creak with the weight. He sat at his desk, it being cluttered with stacks of paperwork, personal items and pictures of his wife. Heth looked at the desktop through haze-filled eyes and rubbed his forehead, attempting to focus and keep the nausea of dizziness from

Chapter Thirteen

moving upward. The desk moved back and forth, but then slowly came into focus. His shaky hand reached out and took a piece of paper from the top of the pile. It was the casualty figures from his division.

His eyes widened as he looked at the amount of men he has lost in the previous day's action. "Fifty percent!" he said to himself, as sickening feeling coming over him. He had not thought that the day's action had been so severe, although he had lay unconscious for twenty-four hours. He called for his captain to return to his tent, he needed all information pertaining to the report that he had just read. The young man folded the tent flaps back before entering, letting the bright sunlight in which caused Heth's eyes to scrunch. His head began to pound again from the light.

"Sir?"

"What happened yesterday? I just looked at the figures, half my men, Captain. Half?" he yelled causing him to shut his eyes from the nausea.

"Sir, we formed on poor ground. The enemy had superior weapons, good ground and gained infantry support."

"This is incredulous. I cannot believe that our casualties were that high. Captain could there be a mistake?"

"Yes, sir. I suppose, the uh.....the count could be slightly... higher."

Heth's eyes widened and his mouth gaped open in disbelief. He hung his head in his hands, thinking about his failure, how his shoe expedition had turned into a bloody conflict. He looked up, slowly shaking his head in bewilderment. "I have failed," he said softly, looking into the distance.

"What, sir?"

"Nothing. Very well, I shall be going to General Lee's."

Heth stood and wavered for a few seconds before his equilibrium settled, then slowly began to walk outside. The sun burst even greater. Squinting he almost closed his eyes in attempting to readjust to the light. His retinas began to constrict so he could see, and he unsteadily walked to his horse. With great effort and crescendoing pain he mounted his horse, then gave instructions to his aides. Heth rode toward Lee's headquarters, brooding the loss of his men deep in his mind.

****

General John Buford sat at his makeshift desk of empty ammunition cases. His office was in his saddle he believed, always in the field. Placing his hand to his head he gently rubbed the rough fingers on his brow. The dull ache that throbbed was a bit annoying, bothersome to him. He pulled a glass bottle out from beside his "desk" and took a swig on the medium brown colored liquid, hoping to dull the pain.

Putting the whiskey bottle away, Buford turned to the papers in front of him. His hand quickly signed parchments and briskly sent them off by one of his aides. Buford sucked in the tantalizing smoke from his pipe and received it into his lungs. Blowing out a long cloud of smoke, he sat back in his chair and began to think.

The old soldiers' motto was to forget the battle by standard of casualties, only to learn from what had happened. Buford sat in the creaking wooden chair and thought on strategy for the new day. The supply chains were a vital necessity of any army. That is what keeps the army alive.

Buford thought deep into the complex nature of supplies. The army is much like a human body, each part having a function. The cavalry are the eyes and ears, seeing and listening to what is in front of them. Supplies. He thought about what area of the body they would be. It came to him and he smiled to himself. Quartermaster and supply were the heart of the army. They supplied the body with what they needed to keep moving. The heart beats and pumps blood through the veins and arteries and delivers that blood to the

Chapter Thirteen

rest of the body. The blood carries oxygen plus the vitamins and nutrients that muscles and organs had to have to stay alive. Supply.

Now to keep the body moving, there needs to be a supply line, which needs to be protected. Buford looked at the sheets in front of him. They were the orders of where to send his men. He began to divide them between his brigade commanders.

Standing to his feet, he felt a bit worn and sore from the previous day. *Perhaps running up and down the stairs*, he thought. Taking a few steps to his right he began to rigorously pace in front of his horse. He needed to be on the move, couldn't sit still when there was anything to do. In fact, Buford found it hard to sit still when there was nothing to do. Orders had to be given, action to be taken. The supply lines would be crucial to the army's victory in this battle. He wanted to be on the front line, to be in the hot sticky heat of war.

Buford looked at his horse and slapped his gloves against his thigh. Donning the faded white leather gloves, he put his foot into the stirrup and mounted the majestic animal. He twitched his mustache and kicked the horse, commanding it to move forward.

****

The man's plume on his hat waved and rippled in the air, a slight breeze running through the feather. He sat atop his mount looking through a pair of field glasses, staring at the horizon. The hills seemed to abound for a very long distance, rolling deep and heavy, dark with its green tint. The other men stared at this man, his bushy heavy beard and striking young features. He stood in his saddle, attempting to see something. Anything.

"Sir.....General Stuart, sir? We have a rider approaching us, sir."

The general said nothing, only pulled his glasses down and looked blankly at the approaching rider.

The rider galloped down the dusty dirt path, earth flying through the air as he came upon the general. He pulled back on the reins, a bit too hard, and the horse whinnied and reared up. The man was a noticeably avid rider as he held on to the horse with ease.

"Sir, I have a report from General Lee. He has instructed you to return to the line at once. The army has been engaged at Gettysburg," the rider said.

"Gettysburg...I see Corporal. Thank you. Give General Lee my compliments. I shall be there today, at once."

J.E.B. Stuart took off his hat and withdrew a handkerchief from his tunic. He dabbed and wiped his forehead, which dripped with sweat from the heat. His nerves began to swell up from the thoughts in his mind, but he quickly quashed them. Lee would not be upset; he had taken over a hundred wagons and ridden around the entire Union Army three times. No, Lee would be impressed, not mad.

Stuart spurred his horse and began to backtrack toward the small town. It was unexpected to have to turn around, and he knew it was unusual for Lee to send for him. Perhaps he was upset. He quickly turned the thought around to shake off that line of thinking. He rode west, the sun beating on his back, sweat pouring from his skin, the stench of war preluding him.

****

Meade walked around his desk, fearing they had been drawn into a battle for which he was not ready. He began to regret taking command, began to wonder if it was the right choice. Everybody was looking at him, cursing under

Chapter Thirteen

his breath, he looked at the reports. No matter how often Hancock reassured him that his was good ground, he worried.

Just taking over, Meade was not prepared for a full out engagement. He swore at Buford for getting him into this, pulling him into battle. Men were talking, bounding around, taking orders as he gave them. He knew they were speaking about him, but Meade didn't care.

He knew the South would attack today, he could feel it. Meade wondered if the ground was good enough, if the troops were stable. He began to think about pulling out, no he couldn't do that. Not after being selected for the job. Reinforce the left, that was what he needed to do. He wasn't going to leave Sickles out there by himself. Those rocky hills....he looked at the maps. Little and Big Round Tops. They needed to secure those heights. If he could get cannons up there...yes, that was it. Protect the left.

"Captain, I need to get a message to all reserves and General Sickles on the double.

****

"Where is he?" belted Buford. "Where is Captain Spalding?"

"We don't know sir," replied Gamble. "Last we saw of him was Gettysburg."

"I will go back and find him."

"Sir, our orders are to be here to guard the trains in Westminster."

Buford removed his hat, rubbing his head before brushing his hair out of his eyes. Cursing he placed the hat back on his head.

****

General Heth attempted to stand but leaned on a tree listening to General Lee talk about fishhooks, rocky hills and the position of the Union. Heth could not pay attention with his eyes fluttering and the sharp aching pain in his head. After the briefing Lee approached Heth, sympathy in his eyes. "General, please go lie down," said Lee.

"Sir I have a division to look after."

"I will assign General Pettigrew to your division. He is second in command and is a fine man."

"Sir, I can be of service."

"I need you General. I cannot spare your services to this army. Please rest with your men. All of your men need rest."

"Yes, sir."

****

General Meade pushed his horse a little harder, Old Baldy twisting his head giving the General a small look of annoyance. Meade rode up to men running around him.

"General, get out of here. There's too much action here sir."

"Action does not concern me. Someone direct me to General Sickles."

"He's over there, sir."

Meade galloped his horse to the dismounted Sickles attempting to calm the hordes of men running past him. "General Sickles!" yelled Meade. "Get over here right now!"

"General Meade," began Sickles. "I am trying to rally the men on, General. I will push these rebels away!"

"General I told you specifically to stay in position on the ridge and you have blatantly disobeyed my command. Now get yourself back on that ridge where you have the high ground," Meade was now screaming, a vein coming out from the side of his head.

"I was taking the fight to them, I felt…"

Chapter Thirteen

"You felt wrong. Get on your horse and tell them to rally on the hill where I placed you last night."

"Sir…"

"Get back now! I have all the rights in the world to court martial you where you stand. Now either get back to the line where I placed you or I promise you, as God as my witness, I will send your butt to the brig for disobeying a direct order. I do not care who you are or how big your family is, now move!"

"Yes, sir."

****

General Pettigrew stepped into the cobblestone home that Lee headquartered himself in. "General Lee, excuse my interruption but General Hill requested me." Hill and Lee returned the salute that Pettigrew greeted them with.

"No apologies General," replied Lee. He turned to Hill, "Do you need the room General?"

"No sir," Hill replied and then looked at Pettigrew. "I am informing you that I want you to temporarily take over for General Heth while he is down from his wound."

"I am honored sir," bowed Pettigrew. "I accept the position with the intentions of not letting you down."

"I know you will not let us down General. I am not asking for anything fancy. I am only asking that you give this army, this country and God all the attention it needs of you at this very moment."

Chapter Fourteen

Ephesians 4:3

Endeavoring to keep the unity of the Spirit in the bond of peace.

July 2, 1863

James stood there his eyes glassed over staring down the barrel of the pistol which pointed at the doctor. His finger slowly began to pull down on the trigger getting ready to shoot this man that would do nothing for Matt. A small breeze picked up and the foul stench of death invigorated his mind to reality; the sensation of other people dying around him. Lowering his weapon, he fell to his knees and planting his face into the dirt.

"I'm terribly sorry Captain," repeated the surgeon before leaving to go inside the barn.

"Captain?" asked Bill. "Sir, we should get moving. Do you want to mark the body?"

James said nothing, but rose from his bowing position one knee at a time cracking as he did so. Walking over to Matt he pulled out a piece of paper from his shirt writing the name and state on the paper, putting it into his tunic pocket.

Chapter Fourteen

Then on another piece of paper he wrote his own information. Looking at Bill, "You want a piece of paper?"

"Why would I do that sir? We are living."

"We will not make it out of here alive. God does not want us to live, any of us."

They walked away from the scene, neither one of them speaking. Silently they worked out in their own heads a way to return to their division, to find a way back to the men who went on without them. They heard there was a place for stragglers who were away from their units. They made their way in the direction of the center of the Union line where strangers congregated.

Walking along the side of a road away from the hospital they saw a body propped up against a tree, not moving.

"You think he's dead?" asked James.

"I think he might be."

The man's eyes flipped open and the light caused the retinas to contract. The blue sky hung over top of him, suspended in the atmosphere. Large white clouds slowly floated by as the wind blew a gentle breeze through the tall grass. The world slowed as the man gazed upon the creation from heaven. His eyes were suddenly shaded by a man standing over him.

The man arose, the world spinning about him, causing nausea to form in his stomach. The side of his head throbbed from every beat of the heart. A large red mark had formed and was visibly noticeable to the men. Eyes blinking rapidly, he tried to focus on the world.

"You ok mister?"

"Yeah, just hit in the head earlier in the day. Stopped here to rest."

"What unit you with?" asked James.

"115th Pennsylvania but don't rightly know where they are now Captain."

"Well come with us because we are going to a place where stragglers go in order to find their units."

They made their way through the dense trees and came out to the field behind the hill. Spotting a courier, they watched a dust trail follow quickly behind as the animal's hooves clopped along. The rider came fast and pulled back hard on the reins, causing the horse to skid to a halt.

"Sir, I have been riding hard all afternoon!"

"Go on, Sergeant."

"The enemy has attacked Little Round Top in force. They have almost turned the lines!"

"Very well," replied James confused.

The sergeant trotted off and left the three to move toward their destination. They headed north towards, what was called, Culp's Hill, just off the Culp family farm. The afternoon sun was beating heavily down upon their faces. The red mark on James' face and throat began to turn a shade of blue, crusted over with dirt and blood. They headed for a farm and were given horses to ride.

As the men rode up the road, the trails of war entered their eyes. Farmhouses had been made into hospitals all along the road. The wounded were carried on stretchers, some hobbled their way in, others crawled. The blood of the Union seemed to flow as a river running for open waters. Confederate prisoners were being led away toward Union headquarters. The wounded enemy lay in the grass, waiting to be attended to. Limbs were piled like firewood, bodies thrown into shallow graves. The men cried out to God, praying for relief, some pleading to die. The more fortunate soldiers were put under the shade of tall oak trees, but there were too many, a hoard of men too great to attend to.

James rode solemnly past the grizzly sights of doctors cutting legs off out in the open air of the day. The stench of bowels, death and decaying flesh filled the humid day, nauseating the captain. A tear formed in the corners of his eye,

Chapter Fourteen

all while the low rumble of distant artillery reminded him of his objective.

Spurring his horse to trot to the lead position, he positioned himself in front of the ammunition wagons. The canvas cover flapped in the wind as the silence of war deafened their eardrums. There was as eerie calm about the day. Dust funnels kicked up on the road and leaves tussled in the afternoon breeze. His eyes darted around, looking at each object blowing in the wind.

Slowly they picked up men, some officers, some enlisted.

His horse pulled at the reins, a bit annoyed at how long they had been riding. Spalding knew that his equestrian friend was tired, but realized resting the horse was not an option. He had to push it a bit longer. He slapped the reins against the animal's neck attempting to tell it to keep going. His thighs were chaffing and knees sore from being bent around the thick ribs of his mount.

"Sir, how much longer are we going today?" asked Bill.

"We need to find the center, I figure we might get information on Culp's hill. Seems like all the fighting is going on up there. They could be overrun too."

"And if that happens the flank caves in and we could lose the line, correct?"

"Absolutely."

"Sir, do you think we have a shot here? I mean, is it worth dying for?"

"Is what worth dying for?"

"All of this." Bill said waving his hand through the air indicating the land around them.

"If you mean this particular town, then yes. This town is our country. It is our land. But it represents so much more than that. It shows the very essence of what this country stands for. Look at these hospitals we are passing. These are the homes of families who live here. They have banded together to help in a common cause. Not because they have chosen to or even wanted to. This particular challenge has been thrust upon them. Nonetheless they have risen and given aid to their fellow man.

"That is what we fight for, one another. We fight to prove that men are men regardless of the appearance of their skin. They are men by the contents of their hearts. This is the very essence of why I am fighting. I cannot speak for other men as to the reason they fight. I fight for my wife. I fight for the lives of men who cannot fight for themselves. For those who are unable to stand against the powers that have oppressed them. I fight for the will of God."

The three men rode in silence for a long time, listening to the chatter of war. The language becoming more recognizable the closer they crept to the battle lines. The closer they came to the battle, the more they saw the horrors of combat.

Splintered trees lined the wood line, bodies scattered throughout the fields. Cannon with one wheel missing, covered wagons strewn about the ground. Caissons tilted to the ground unattached to anything to pull them. Rivers of men flowing to and fro. The blood lines of war spurting in and out of hell. Lives to be taken, blood to be lost. All in all, another day in the life of a soldier in battle.

The hooves of the horse clomped on the dirt road beneath. The third man began to speak to James about his own children and wife. "They have the most beautiful green eyes, all of them. My wife and daughter, they have gorgeous blond hair. The little one has some curls but just a hint. Sir, I ain't seen another woman like my wife. Whooo wee, she's a beaut. She is the prettiest woman in my town. No one thought we would ever get together, but she fell for me. Of course, it did take some persuadin'"

"How so?"

"I practically had to beg her," he said chuckling. James pulled three cigars out of his tunic, handed one to each of his comrades. "She laughed so hard at my pleading, I guess she

Chapter Fourteen

felt sorry for me. I started courtin' her and well I guess she fell for me."

"Hmm." James puffed on his thick brown cigar.

"Yes, sir. She sure is a beautiful woman. My daughter looks just like her, gonna grow up to be gorgeous. She will make some man so happy one day. Can't wait to see that little girl grow up. That, sir, is why I fight. So I can go home and see my daughter. My son, he's another story. I hear he just started walkin'. Sure sorry I missed that. But anyhow, he won't stop walking around the cabin. My wife keeps chasin' him down. I guess that's how she keeps that figger of hers. When I left he was starting to crawl, squealing all the time. He looks more like me, dark hair, tough chin. He'll sure be a lady killer." Bill snickered a little.

The cannon fire that was in the distance was no longer far away as Culp's Hill was now in sight. Fence rows were lying strewn over the sod, resting soldiers underneath shading trees. The battle glazed eyes of men looked at the passing assemblage of supplies. A breeze began to lightly blow, moving the stench of the dead that lay on the side of the road away from their noses for a brief moment. Flies swarmed around the sun beaten bodies as they laid motionless in the ditches.

Enemy artillery began to pour into the ground ahead of them. Musket fire filled the air with the sound of popping and the odor of gun powder. The wheels on the wagon crunched along the gravel and bounced over rocks and holes. The sound of rickety wood was heard over the din of battle.

James and the men made their way to an artillery line close to Culp's Hill. As they passed behind them, they began to fire their twelve pound Napoleon guns. One by one, these weapons boomed their loud deep voices. Clouds of smoke puffed out from their long black barrels. Bill began to ride up next to one of the guns. He was speaking to an artilleryman.

Upon The Eastern Sun

Turning to look at the wagon train behind, James was startled by a loud explosion to his left. He spun his head around in time to see Bill's horse rearing up and throw him from its back. James sat up in his saddle, the leather creaking, his hand covering his brow as he struggled to see the man through the fog of smoke. Eyes squinting, he called out his name.

With a kick of his spurs, the metal dug into the ribs of the steed. The hind legs kicked and James jaunted over to the exploded cannon. Limbs and ligaments strewn about the area caused him to cringe with nausea. There he found his friend, lying on the ground, eyes to the heavens. Leaping from his horse, boots hitting the dirt causing sod to spill over his heals, he called out.

"Bill!" he yelled as he ran as fast as he could, his feet seemed to barely touch the ground. He skidded to a halt on his knees, grass and dirt staining his slacks. "Bill, are you alright?"

"I'm fine but must have landed on my back wrong or something...I can't...I can't feel my legs." he said deeply huffing in air.

"Bill," James replied in a whisper, hand upon the man's neck, "you sure do seem to have landed wrong." Swallowing the lump in his throat, he continued, "I think you may have broken something, that's why you can't feel anything."

"I can't move my arms, sir. What does this mean? Am I gonna die, Captain?"

"I...I'm afraid...I don't know."

"Sir, there's a letter in my tunic pocket. I didn't have time to send it to my wife. If I do die, can you see that she gets it, sir?"

Unbuttoning the tunic that Bill no longer could, he took out the letter. "You will deliver this for me, won't you Captain. Please James." He nodded, tears blinding him,

Chapter Fourteen

streaks running down his face. "Tell them to keep me here. I like this tree....don't let them move me Captain."

"I tell you...I don't wanna die.. please dear God, I don't wanna die. I love my daughter and boy. I can't die, please Lord don't let me pass on." His eyes became heavy closing into darkness. "Sweetheart? Sweetie? I'm home. I'm.... home."

"Bill?" James whispered, "Bill!" He was now yelling, his voice cracking. His chest heaved up and down as he wept bitterly, knowing it was for Matt whom he cried. A river poured from his eyes, dripping onto Bill's dirt and blood stained blue uniform. James beat the man's chest, throwing his hat to the ground. Withdrawing the fallen man's sword, he viciously beat the tall oak tree next to him. Slashing, cutting and stabbing at the dark brown bark that thickly covered the tree. Chips of bark began to fall to the ground. He continued until he slumped to the earth in exhaustion.

The men whom he had joined watched the sight before them. "Captain...we pushed on ahead of you. The supplies seem to be flowing all over the place but we found where the exact center is, sir. We will return to camp."

James stared off with glassy eyes into the distance, off into the horizon.

"Sir?"

"Very well, but help me with this man." Kneeling once more over the body, he buttoned the tunic from where he had taken the letter. He reached his hand into his own left breast pocket and removed the letter. He felt the rough parchment in his hands, kneading his finger back and forth upon it. He sniffed loudly and put the paper back into his pocket. The two men lifted Bill's motionless body and laid it underneath the tree.

The sun was slowly dying over the Blue Ridge Mountains, raising colors brightly shining over the hill bound range surrounding Gettysburg. James and the others rode slowly, mournful steps proceeding them. Horses weary from the long day of riding drudged along, soldiers tired and aching from battle held their heads down at the passing of the day as well as their friend.

Riding in silence, no one spoke to James. Riding in front of the wagon containing bodies of other men, his face was like a painting. The expressionless statue of him caused men to scrunch their brows, either in question or in understanding. His body was motionless except for the movement upon his mount. The eerie sounds of battle lines in the distance reminded the men the battle was not over, perhaps was just beginning.

The line of mismatched men reached camp when darkness was just about to overtake the light. A colonel sat in his creaking wooden chair, smile upon his face when James rode in. He slowly dismounted and trudged up to the colonel.

"Captain, anything I can help you with?"

"Sir, we have all been detached from our units and are looking for a place to camp and find our regiments.

"I understand. Have you many casualties?"

"Yes, sir. Many along the way to this position, one I had just met and one whom I cared for deeply."

"Dear God. Get some rest, we will speak again in the morning."

"Yes, sir," James said as he saluted and turned away.

"Oh, and Captain?"

"Yes, sir?"

"I am sorry."

"Yes, sir."

Walking back to his horse, he saw her being attended by other caregivers. The horse was cooling down before being able to take a drink. Spalding began to unbuckle the saddle. He turned and saw four men taking lifeless bodies away for burial. Turning back to his horse, he stripped the blanket off her back and began to brush her in a therapeutic motion,

Chapter Fourteen

slowly stroking her brown hair. She drank from a bucket, sloshing the water down her dry itchy throat. An aide came and set a pail of oats down for her to eat. Her nose guided her to the pail and she began to munch.

After he had finished brushing her, James had a stablehand finish the care of his horse. He walked into a tent and lay upon a cot, eyes staring at the canvas above him. Small tears began to form out of the corners of his eyes and ran down his temples, stopping in this thick blond hair.

James fumbled around his thick blue coat and found the letter Bill had wanted him to deliver. He tossed it on a dark oak desk and watched it slide up against a Bible. He stared at the black leather bound book for a moment before reaching for it.

"Show me something God. Tell me that you're real." he hoarsely whispered to himself. He slowly opened the pages and it fell open upon his lap. *Precious in the sight of the Lord is the death of his saints.* His lips began to tremble, rage coursing through his veins. He stood to his feet and violently threw the book toward the ground, kicking it into the air. The pages rapidly blew from the force, landing outside the opening of the tanned colored tent. An orderly walking by saw James lay back down on his cot. The young man picked up the black Bible and walked away. "I knew you weren't real!" James yelled.

The day drew to a close with the sound of rifles in the distance, the occasional howl of a dog and the cries of the wounded resonated through the air. The heat drew more lightening in the sky as men sat around fires, playing cards, sipping on whiskey or playing a banjo and guitar. Laughter spread about the camp, as morale from the day reigned high about the pines and oaks of the land.

"You see debts are suppose to be paid, it's that simple," one man was speaking in the group.

"But with this war, many debts will go unpaid. We can't expect every debt to be paid," said another.

"Romans 13:8 states, 'Let no debt remain outstanding,'" the first man retorted.

"Yes, but Deuteronomy 15:1 states 'seven years you must cancel our debt'," the second man piped back.

"Matthew 6:12 says 'Forgive us our debts," a third person chimed in.

James merely walked past the conversation sitting down on a stump with his other companion, collar unbuttoned on his sweat stained shirt. He was sipping from his flask and allowing the substance to sit in his mouth, swishing it around a little before allowing the burn to flow down his throat into his stomach to warm it. Silence now filled the air, the previous conversation on hold, as the men listened to the crackle of the fire and watched the flames flicker about the round base of the fire. No man spoke, not knowing what to say.

The crickets acted as singers to the guitar and banjo playing in the camp, mosquitoes buzzed in the men's ears whispered to them. Still no one said a word, silence being the predominant conversation at hand.

"Heard them rebs might attack agin in the mornin'," the man broke the silence. "Heard they were goin' to try and flank the army. Go 'round 'em to the right or sumethin' like that!"

"Don't believe everything you hear," replied James.

"Rumors do like to fly. I guess that's how we git intelligence reports," chuckled the man. The men laughed and the tension eased slightly. "Well, I hear them rebs are comin' right up the center."

"Ha! That would be suicide. Look at that field in front. No, General Lee would not send troops through that. We would though!" laughed James.

The laughter around the campfire was louder and with each burst came the loosening of the belt of nerves, guards

Chapter Fourteen

being let down. James sat and listened to the men, not saying another word, just sipping on his flask of scotch.

Cigar smoke began to blend with the fire causing the night sky to be filled with the smoky aroma of sweet tobacco mixed with musky cherry. The nostrils of each man inhaled the scent forever burned into their minds when they would smell the fragrance again. Forever would they remember where they were when they smelled it. The conversations repeatedly changed topics, men pointing two fingers containing cigar or pointing pipes at each other. From war to love, back to war, to hunting, then again back to war. Strategies flew about, each man knowing how to end the war, knowing what was best for the Union. From trapping techniques to dance steps, everybody chimed in. All but James.

He would smirk once in a while, chuckle slightly at times, but never would he speak. The night grew old and died, another day being born. The subject of war at hand again, then it changed to religion and faith.

"We haven't seen an army as great as the Potomac since the Roman days!" cried one officer, causing men to scoff.

"I certainly do hope that was a joke. They put Jesus to death," said another.

"It had to happen. To fulfill prophecy and save the world," retorted the first.

"Anybody bin to California?"

"Where did that come from?"

"I've bin," said the officer. "I was there with Hancock, the General, but he was a captain there. You know who else was there? Armistead. Major Armistead. Best friends they were. Armistead now is a general too, only for the South. Beautiful relationship they had, so very close. Didn't think they would ever be separated, but the war did. Separated many of us."

"That's the great deceit of war. Everybody gets caught up in their cause, they don't see the consequences of the decision," said a different man. He went on, "Never have so many died, each with a cause in their hearts. Families are torn, friends ripped apart, and yet the flag of cause is raised high. When the dust clears and the fires die, what cause will there be then? Eventually our causes die right alongside our men, then what do we have? Innocence? That dies. We have lost so much, how do we recover?"

"I fought in the Mexican War and then went west 'gainst them Indians," said the unknown officer. "How we move on or recover is the only way we live. The memories and nightmares will follow us for the rest of our lives, but we move on. We bury our dead and let them rest, we don't carry their bodies with us, just the memory of their lives. We carry the good and try and block the bad. We do move on. It takes time and prayer. I've spent many a night up in prayer, guided only by the moonlight. God is with us, that is how we recover."

James sat on the stump trying to take in the words, but they couldn't sink in. His heart wouldn't allow the brain to absorb the words and their meanings. The sorrow had turned to anger and then to bitterness. Hatred slowly seeping in, turning the love to black. The darkness of the night was deep in his mind, slowly taking control.

"I'd like to raise a toast to our fallen comrades. Great men, officers and soldiers." The others agreed and held their drink high about them. "All things happen for God's will, even death. Wouldn't you agree Captain Spalding?"

He looked at the men by the glow of the fire in his eyes. "What God?"

Chapter Fifteen

Revelation 1:18

...behold, I have the keys of hell and of death.

July 2, 1863

The sword swung high in the air, the blade gleaming in the sun, reflecting the light of the late afternoon glow. The man's gray sleeve waved back and forth as he gave the command to move forward. His rough beard swayed from the movement of his jaw as he yelled.

The troops poured forward toward the weak Union line, held up by the formation of rocks at the base of Little Round Top. Musket fire screamed through the air as cannons boomed. Minie balls flew about striking rocks, trees and men. A shot came from the rocky tree line and struck the man in the left arm.

His sword circled in the air, falling down, thumping on the ground. The boots on his feet slipped out of the stirrups and his body fell to the sod below him. He rolled over looking to the blue sky above, partially blocked by large green leaves gently swaying in the breeze. A sharp pain extended down from his shoulder to his left hand.

"General Hood!" a young lieutenant yelled, running up to the general then crouching down beside the man. The world began to slow, arms being pointed in different directions in a slow motion voice seemingly far away. Hood turned his head watching men come with a stretcher, setting it on the ground next to him. Two men picked up the general and placed him on the stretcher.

"Take him to the hospital behind our lines. Get the doctor immediately!"

Hood lay on the litter watching the trees pass slowly, while seeing the ground strewn with men. Limbs passed his sight just as timber flows down a river current. This grizzly sight caused his stomach to turn and his eyes to close. He bounced along, atop the stretcher, waiting on what the surgeon would have to do.

****

His beard stood stiff in the light breeze, hands rubbing his eyes. He hoped once his fingers and palms slid down his face the horrific scene would disappear. When he removed his guard the sight remained. Men were screaming and yelling at the top of their lungs, which filled his ears with such deafening roar it caused him to cringe.

"At what cost was this cause worth? How much can we endure?" he thought to himself. "Too much carnage, too many dead. How many sons of the South have to die? How many mountains of limbs must be given?"

"Sir?" the man interrupted his thought, "General Sir, General Hood has been shot."

"Oh my. I wish to go see him," replied Pettigrew.

The doctor turned in his once white, now red smock that covered his body. Pettigrew followed him, walking through the maze of bodies. He stepped over sun-blistered men, sweat and rotting flesh mixed in the air.

Chapter Fifteen

He entered the white and gray barn and into a stall where Hood was laying on a stretcher, propped up on some logs. Hood's eyes fluttered as he struggled with consciousness, attempting to stay awake to speak.

"Are you and the general close sir?"

"No. Just a fellow general."

"Yes sir."

"Your boys did good, Sam. You just rest. General Heth, General Archer, and now General Hood," Pettigrew stated.

"At what cost?"

****

His boots thumped along the wooden floor, the boards creaking as the weight of his body pressed down upon them. Heth paced back and forth, left hand down at his side, right hand scratching his beard. He paced along the front porch of a home he did not know. He left his tent in order to gain fresh air but his brain was dizzy with thoughts and pain. His mind raced with impetuous thoughts, electrons streaming and neurons firing continuously and simultaneously.

"Sir, more reports from the hill outside Gettysburg," interrupted Major Finney.

"The rocky ore. We took it, Dear God say we took it."

"No sir. The report is from the hill by the Culp farm."

"Go on Major."

"Sir, the attack is winding down but...but we were unable to push them back."

Heth said nothing but paused slightly in his pacing before turning around. The soles of his boots crackled and scraped the dust and dirt ridden floor of the gray slated stone house. His head fell down, chin touching his chest, before collapsing into a wooden rocking chair.

"Sir! General Heth, sir!"

"I am quite all right Major. Just tired and frustrated. These attacks were supposed to begin at the same time. I heard that this morning, did I hear wrong Major?"

"General, all commanders knew their job. They recognized the importance of duel flank attacks, sir."

"I do not understand. I do not know why they were not executed properly. The flank was supposed to cave, supposed to give way. Dear Lord, I do not understand your methods at times."

"Sir?"

"Nothing, Major. Please allow me to be with my thoughts."

"Yes, sir." The steps creaked with the weight of each foot as Major Finney left the porch and walked up the street.

Heth sat in a stranger's chair, "Heavenly Father. What is happening? This is not what I expected, this is not what I thought You wanted." Heth tapped his finger on the banister top, his head down, eyes closed. "Too many have died. Too many lost. At what price, dear Lord, do we....do we continue? At what cost do we gain victory? Your children wandered in the desert for forty years because of their stubbornness. Do not make us like the Israelites. Please God, bring us to the promised land."

A small tap on the porch post interrupted Heth's thoughts and Finney's head peered through the porch railings. "Sir, I apologize, but General Pettigrew is being quite persistent upon seeing you."

"Let him in Major."

Pettigrew entered, holding his hat in his left hand, saluting with the right. Returning the salute, Heth sat down in his rocking chair, the joints rubbing against each to cause the creaking noise that resonated throughout the room.

"Sir. I report from the right flank. We were unable to push the Yanks off that little rocky hill." Heth remained silent, just staring at the map on his table. "Sir, General Hood was hit

Chapter Fifteen

in the arm. Doctor said he is going to lose it. I did see him at the hospital."

"Which arm?"

"The left one Sir."

"Jackson lost his right." Heth stated under his breath.

"Sir?"

"Nothing. General, we are losing far too many commanders. I feel as if we are out of God's grace sometimes. Too many men have died, too many body parts lost. I'm tired...so very tired."

"Sir, we still have a chance. We can still win this battle. We have great men and a great deal of spirit to work with. Our boys are rested and feeling better each passing minute. We will regain the advantage from today. I feel it. I have confidence in our boys I truly do."

"Hood is a great man."

"Sir?" Pettigrew looked at Heth with the scrunched brows and narrowed eyes of confusion. He turned to exit the house, now understanding that because of his injury, General Heth was not yet able to comprehend the full extent of the day.

****

The man picked up a brush from the wooden bucket, metal bands surrounding the outside rims. He gently began to brush his brown mare, starting with the left side of her body. He used circular motions beginning at the neck, slowly working toward her withers. He moved down the shoulder, lifting up dirt, loose hair and dead skin. He brushed along the length of her body, downward across her barrel and then to her croup.

"General Stuart?"

"Yes, Corporal?"

"General Lee is sending for you sir."

Upon The Eastern Sun

"Very well," replied Stuart throwing the brush at the young stocky brunette corporal. "Finish for me." He straightened his plumed hat and smoothed out his beard and mustache. His thick beard flew in the wind as he stepped outside the barn. His mustache extended out past his beard pointing at his shoulders. The hat on his head curled and buttoned at the left edge, the other contained the plume. It rose slightly, rounding off at the top, with a bowl like dip at the peak and center.

As Stuart walked toward Lee's headquarters, he saw gloomy eyes looking at him. His stomach churned a bit, nerves eating at his esophagus. One fateful step in front of the other, his knee-high, black leather riding boots crunching along the gravel. His sword made a clanging noise as it hit his left hip and leg.

Stopping outside the slate gray house, he saw Lee pacing while talking to Major Taylor. Lee stopped and pointed at a map laying on the table then continued pacing. Stuart remained motionless, eyes wide, thoughts streaming through his mind. The main thought being of remorse. He had gone on a mission to satisfy his thirst, his damaged ego. He knew this to be true and his thoughts about that continued to be on his mind.

Taylor exited the side door and saw Stuart. "Ah, General Stuart. I will let General Lee know you are here."

"Thank you Major." Stuart watched him enter the house again then reappear.

"You may go in General."

Stuart said nothing but entered the house. He latched the door behind him and removed his hat. He extended a salute, waiting for Lee to return it. Lee hesitated but then returned the salute. Stuart's hand slowly dropped, knowing that he had upset Lee.

"What was your mission General Stuart?"

"Sir?"

Chapter Fifteen

"What instructions did I give to you? What was your job?"

"To scout out enemy movements, to report to you about the Union whereabouts, sir."

"You failed."

"After I spoke with you sir I spoke with General Longstreet as well. His orders were vague sir. I felt I was doing what I was instructed. I had no real orders sir…"

"I do not expect a retort from you of that sort! I expect you to listen."

Stuart said nothing, but his eyes grew wide, eyebrows rose and forehead wrinkled in question.

"You left this army with nobody watching out for us. Do you know who we tangled with the first day of battle? Of course you do not. You were not here. It was Union cavalry; the very same people you were suppose to keep occupied. I have had to use, God forgive me, spies to give me enemy position and movements. I trusted you General Stuart, more than most of my commanders." Stuart continued to stand at a semi-attention state, no words coming from his mouth. "I have known you for some time now. I have trusted you for a long time.

"I trusted you in 1859 when we fought John Brown and I trusted you to this campaign. You have let me down. I am quite disappointed in your actions."

"Sir, allow me to explain."

"There is no explanation General," bellowed Lee.

"Yes, sir."

"You are dismissed. I will give you orders later, for now rest your men and yourself."

Stuart stepped outside the house and fixed his hat on his head. He looked up at the night sky, darkness above him. A small tear formed in his left eye and fell upon his thick mustache.

****

"You lost, soldier?"

"Just looking for my unit sir. We was in a hell of a fight earlier. Don't know where anybody is. What unit is this?"

"Battery B, Fourth U.S. Artillery and I'm Captain Michael Wiedrich, across the way there is Captain Rickett's battery. Sit down son, you look exhausted."

"Thank you, sir. You been in any action today, sir?"

"No doesn't look as though we will either. What's your name, son? Your unit?"

"Oh, I'm sorry, sir. I'm Private Jeremiah Jenson, sir. I'm with the 115th Pennsylvania."

"How did you get turned around?"

"Not from this part of the state. Just got lost somehow. Glad I ran into you, sir."

"Well, you're more than welcome to stay here for the time being. Sun's going down. Find your outfit in the morning," Wiedrich said, turning to his aide. "Sergeant, get this young man some coffee please."

"Yes, sir," the sergeant said, turning and walking toward the fire.

"Sir. Can I ask you a question?"

"Go ahead, son."

"Did you see anything that happened today?"

"Well, not too much. Received some artillery damage earlier in the day, sometime around four this afternoon. We fired back at them, forward scouts said we made them move back. That's been about it."

"We saw plenty yesterday. Arrived late but saw many a good man die. Saddens me." The sound of distant cannon fire broke the conversation. "Where's that comin' from?"

"That would be a lot of fighting to the right of us. That's Culp Hill. It could be a diversion. I want you to stick around here. If you need ammunition see the sergeant. Stick around

Chapter Fifteen

the C.P. If you would. I feel a whole lot of scrapin' coming this way." Wiedrich turned and rushed to his cannoneers, giving instructions and waving his hand.

"We are the forward gunners," he said to his men. "Behind us Battery B and others from the 4th U. S. Artillery. They will be in support of us, but we must not let them overtake this position. Load your cannons with canister shot. I have a feeling they will come directly in front of us. That fire to the right of us is not the only assault. Now move out, load up and fire when commanded. I tell you the truth gentlemen, it will get distasteful here. Hold on to your guns. Move out!"

Wiedrich hastily walked back to his tent and put on his black leather belt. The sword clanged and struck his knee. His hands shook as he tried to fasten the buckle. He breathed through his nostrils, flaring them as he exhaled. Chest rising heavily and rapidly, he straightened his blue jacket. He threw open his tent flap and saw the line of blue coats at a stone wall open fire into the distance. Lifting his head a little higher and squinting he saw the long gray line.

"Set cannons, make ready to fire when commanded!" yelled the captain.

Cannons opened fire to the rear of him as the sun slowly sank to their left. Wiedrich pulled out his field glasses then quickly pulled them from his eyes, returning them to their brown hard leather case. The darkness that was setting in before him caused him not to be able to see everything, but the late sun caused just enough light to show that the remnants of XI Corps were falling back.

The rebel yell burst above the atrocious noise of battle like a banshee in the midst of night. It caused the small hairs on the back of Wiedrich's neck to tingle. Small bands of Union soldiers strayed past his cannons.

"Hold fast boys, hold fast! Rally on us, rally!" The gray coats of the Confederate Army reached a firing position and

Wiedrich gave the command to fire. "Open fire! Reload and fire at will!"

The canister shot poured out of the barrel of the twelve pound Napoleon cannons. The cans burst open revealing the lead shot that spread throughout the gray line. The lead balls ripped through the clothes and flesh of the rebels and some Union. The lines intermingled, rifles and bayonets being swung at each other.

Cannons from the U. S. 4th Artillery opened up and began to tear through the enemy and friendly soldiers. Wiedrich fired his pistol, cocking it back each time taking aim then firing. The rebel line was no longer a line, just a blur of soldiers. He continued to attempt to find his way in the dark, squinting his eyes. Two southern flags were planted in front of him, near his guns, as he fired his last round.

Holstering his six shot pistol and unsheathing his sword, Wiedrich slashed and stabbed at the enemy. His movements swift and articulated. A long bearded gray soldier came rushing at him from his left. Wiedrich's head turned, his sword still lodged in the belly of another. The enemy lifted his rifle, yielding a bayonet and aimed at the captain's chest. Wiedrich's eyes grew wide, heart beating faster and stomach muscles tightening as he cringed.

The man continued to run at Wiedrich, beard bouncing with the motion. A shot from darkness rang out and the bearded man stumbled and fell to his knees. Wiedrich looked behind him and saw Jenson standing there, fixing his bayonet onto his Enfield. The darkness then flashed bright and specks of stars sprinkled in his eyes.

Wiedrich fell to his knees and looked to his left. He saw waves of blue uniforms pouring into the battle and the flag of the 119th New York. His eyes fluttered and his face fell to the ground.

Chapter Sixteen

Colossians 3:1

Since, then, you have been raised with Christ, set your hearts on things above, where Christ is seated at the right hand of God.

July 2, 1863

Meade sifted through the pile of papers sitting on his desk, his knee bobbed up and down with anxiety and anticipation. Every time a horse ran up to the house, acid in his stomach reached his throat. Standing behind the desk, not really looking at the orders and maps in front of him, he tried to look busy.

The loud voice outside overrode the sound of boots on the front porch. He heard the door handle jiggle and squeak as it turned, the wooden aperture opening. Meade's eyes squinted in the lamp lit room as General Hancock strode in, wearing his ever present clean white shirt.

"General Meade, I am here to report."

"Go on Hancock."

"Battle's finally dieing down, last shots were heard a few minutes ago." Hancock said, sitting down in a chair across from Meade. Crossing his legs, he continued, "Around dusk I began to hear a lot of artillery fire on our extreme right. I received many mixed reports, some good, most bad. Knowing how the reports get out of proportion, I decided to send some men over that way. Apparently it was a good decision. I sent Colonel Samuel Carrol of the 1st Brigade to Cemetery Hill, sir.

"There he had the 4th Ohio, 14th Indiana and the 7th West Virginia." continued Hancock. "They poured into dismal lines that were left. Pushed the Rebels back and we retained our lines. We were successful this day, sir."

"Good, good. I have other thoughts about today's win."

"How is that, sir?"

"Our interior lines are weak, uh....they could sweep right around us." Meade swung his arm, then grabbed his side in pain.

"Sir, are you all right?"

"Yes, yes Hancock. Just my injury from Glendale and the battle there. Acts up on me sometimes."

"Yes, sir." Hancock stared at Meade.

"You know, I served under General Taylor or former President Taylor as people would call him now. He taught me two very important lessons. One, watch what you eat," Meade chuckled while Hancock gave a weary smile believing it to be in bad taste, "the other was you can win any battle if you position your troops correctly."

"I agree sir, full heartedly."

"Good. You see we were sort of forced upon this ground. I do not like that. I have been urging other generals and now I will mention it to you. I think we are in a bad position here. Our center is weak and that is the heart of any good line. No matter how strong the flank positions are, if the center folds, an army is divided. We must withdraw and we must do it now. What is your opinion Win?"

"Sir, may I speak freely?"

Chapter Sixteen

"Of course."

" I believe it would be foolhardy to abandon this position. Our flanks are strong, which was proven today. We can get supplies quickly from the trains and wagons. Our interior lines are quite solid, sir, not trying to disagree with you. Yes, our center is weak but sir, a head on attack of that sort would be suicide. We face a mile of open field, artillery on both sides. A full frontal attack would be a mass graveyard. Sir, we put your headquarters here because it was the safest place to be. My opinion is, we stay. If they attack the center, which is highly nonstrategic, we could repel them at once. Sir, if they attack we will prevail."

"Very well. We will stay. It is against my better judgment, but we will do it. Excuse me General Hancock please, I have papers to attend to and orders to fill."

"Of course, sir," Hancock replied rising and left Meade with a desk full of papers and a room full of staff members.

Meade's eyes grew heavy, sleep deeply upon them. They slowly connected with the dark large bags underneath the pupils. His breathing became deeper and his mind transfixed on a distant land, long across the sea.

The breakers crashed upon the shore behind him, giant sea walls engulfed his vision. His brother Richard was ankle deep in the dark salty water, a Spanish family ran up the coastline. His family was ripped apart by war then, as well as now. Breathing becoming faster, his heart increasing in beats. His dream mixed with cannon fire, Richard running from the sea now stained with blood.

"General Meade!" yelled Richard, "General Meade."

Meade opened his eyes to see his aide, not Richard, standing across his desk. "Sir, we need signatures on these ammunition releases."

"Of course, Henry, of course. My apologies, I seemed to have dozed off there. Sit Henry, sit. Did you know that I am an engineer?"

"Yes, sir," Henry said, puzzled by the shift in conversation. "I believe someone told me that once."

"Oh. Well I tell you this. I miss it. I designed many of the lighthouses we see. Some of which those rebs use. Do you believe in God, son?"

Taken aback again by the sudden change in topic the young aide replied, "Firmly, sir."

"Met a man from Michigan once while doing the survey of Lake Michigan. Fascinating man he was. A devout Christian. Solid in his belief. Faith greater than that I have ever see. I wish I had that now. Wish I had his faith."

"Yes, sir. A mustard seed sir."

"What?"

"Nothing, sir. The signature?"

"Yes, yes. Here it is, you may go about your business."

Meade shuffled through his papers, crinkling in his hands. The scratching noise of documents running through fingertips filled the dark room. His rough hands attended to the pen and papers as a surgeon to a patient. Soon the chatter of war would break the silence that arose through the night. Soon the tears of mothers would fill the crater holes of artillery shells. Very soon, the dirt that formed the ground would receive a murky red tint in the form of puddles.

****

Buford threw a three inch thick log on the fire. Ashes blew up into the air, glowing in the night backdrop which slowly fused out into a dark powder. He slowly sat down, his back bent over as he rolled his heels and fell into his wooden chair. Buford stretched out his legs, extending them towards the fire. He put his dark cherry colored pipe to his lips and sucked in the sweet smoke taste of the tobacco. He sighed, removing his hat and set it on an empty ammunition crate that sat next to him.

Chapter Sixteen

"I tell ya Devin, I came from a long tradition of military in my family. A grandfather, Abraham Buford, he was a colonel. A great uncle. They both served in the War of Independence. I have a half brother, Napoleon Bonaparte Buford, he is in the Union. Another cousin, also named Abraham he.. well he went the other way." Buford said in conversation as if he and Devin were already in the midst of one.

"What do you mean, General?"

"He fights for the South. He is a rebel, cavalry too."

"Sir, I do not think that there is a single one of us that does not know someone on the other side."

"Well..it was a little different for me."

"How is that?"

"I am a Kentuckian. My father owns slaves. Most of my wife's family fights for the South. I even got a letter from the Governor of Kentucky saying I could go anywhere I wanted. I...well as you can see turned it down."

"Why Sir? Why did you not fight for the South?"

"Couldn't fight against the country that showed me my passion and gave me my career. I remember looking to two men, Colonel Hanney and Colonel Cooke. They were from the south and they stayed with the Union. I looked up to them."

"We all make decisions that sometimes we do not understand. It is almost as God breathed in our lungs, to force out the words I am saying."

"Could be."

"God must play a hand in the grand scheme of things more than we know. The birth of children....and the death of war. It seems as though he knows the whys, the whens and the wheres. Just does not enjoy telling us."

"Seems so," replied Buford rubbing his knee.

"Knee bothering you again. The one you hurt in Second Bull Run?"

"Yeah...can you believe that damn Union paper, reporting I was dead?" sputtered Buford.

"Actually, yes I can."

"Newspapers will print anything that sells. Any headline and story. Don't have to be true, just anything for circulation increase. I guess everyone is making a buck on this war. Making Union greenbacks off the red blood of soldiers. Off their red back. Disgusts me."

A rider slowly approached the two men sitting by the fire. It crackled a symphony of noise and glimmered a ballet of flames. The two men grew silent, transfixed by the sight in front of them. The rider dismounted and strode up to the two men, the fire illuminating his riding boots.

"Sir, General Hancock wishes to give orders for the morning," said the courier.

"Go on son."

"He wants the train protected as we resupply the flanks."

"Very well, give the General my regards."

"Yes, sir," replied the courier, saluting, mounting his horse and rode off into the darkness.

****

"Sir, shouldn't you get some sleep?"

"Oh, don't you be worrin' about me laddie. I have bin doin' this sort of things before you was born," replied Gamble in his Irish accent. "I am just finishin me letter to my Sophia. Is there something I might be helping you with Private?"

"I keep thinking about the other day, sir, how them rebs kept comin' and comin'. I will be honest sir, it gave me a fright."

"We all be scared in one form or nother. But nonetheless, you performed your job and that 'tis the sign of a good soldier, lad. I wrote an order once to the 8th Illinois, it was. That

Chapter Sixteen

be when I used to command. I said to them, the first duty of a soldier is a prompt and cheerful obedience to all lawful orders and no one is fit to command, in any capacity, who is not hisself willin' to obey.' In that model, which I do believe, you did very well, me lad."

"But how do you calm your fear?"

"Well, laddie, I returned to command less than a month ago."

"Yes sir, you just missed a large engagement of cavalry at Brandy Station. Colonel Davis was killed there sir," replied the private, looking at his boots. "I was scared there too."

"Well, you weren't with me yet but in the Pennsylvania Campaign I was shot in me chest. It skipped off a rib and lodged right here in me back," described Gamble as he stood and pointed to the area of his back. "Two days ago was me first engagement since that day last year."

"Sir, you lead without regard of life."

"I lead because..." Gamble's explanation was interrupted by a loud sneeze. He wiped his nose on his sleeve then lifted his other arm and dabbed his watery eyes. "Excuse me son, I lead because I had to. Me life is not the only one on the field of battle. I lead or people die. It is the same with you young man. If you don't fight many a good lads will die, all the while you are running away."

"I am not a soldier sir. I worked at a feed mill before joining."

"And I, laddie, was a civil engineer in Chicago. Sure, I fought in the Seminole War with the 1st U.S. Dragoons, but I studied back in me home country. Worked in the Queen's surveying office, I did. I'm not anymore a qualified soldier than you, but now what do you think? That was our former lives, now we are soldiers. You, me, even me son George."

"I still cannot believe we won."

"Well now...not quite the victory the high ups were hoping for. But for us, a valiant success. Of course, had it not bin for the breech loaders, I dare say, I would not like to know the outcome."

"I am sorry sir for keeping you up and from your letter. Is there anything you need before I go to sleep?"

"Naw, laddie. Nothing. Rest up, we ride again tomorrow."

The young private closed the beige tent flap behind him and left Gamble to himself. The crickets chattered to each other, telling secrets to themselves. William Gamble rubbed his chest and smiled a little, thinking on his photograph. *Everyone called me crazy*, he thought to himself. He was the only one who had smiled getting their pictures taken that day.

The sound of distant thunder caused him to dim his lamps. The sound of storms reminded Gamble of Ireland. He removed his tunic, unraveled his suspender from his shoulders and lay down on his bunk. He stared up at the top of his tent, the dim light suspended from the canopy flickered and danced about causing shadows to play games with his eyes. His lids became heavy and finally closed.

Chapter Seventeen

◆

Jeremiah 10:23

*I know, O Lord, that a man's life is not his own,
it is not for man to direct his steps.*

July 3, 1863

The crickets sang their lullaby as the fires lie down to take their naps. Joshua slept semi-peacefully, his head resting on his tunic, which was draped over a tree root. His butternut kepi laid upon his chest rising and falling through the air. His heavy breathing gave the illusion of a restful sleep, but his mind did not shut down and replayed the days of horror that he had seen.

His eyes flashed open quick as lightning would dart across a dark sky. The moon was still at work, slowly lowering into day. He blinked a few times before raising his upper torso in a sitting position. He was a bit leery about his surroundings, something felt off, as if God was trying to relay a message to him. He turned over on his knees and began to pray silently.

"My Heavenly Father, I beseech Thee today to pour out Your blessedness upon this company of mine. Father God, for I do not know the plan of our commander General Lee, but be with him. Father keep all these men, raise them in the palm of your hand. Protect them and their families with your mighty angels. Reveal this day to me Father, reveal this conflict. Spiritually, heavenly, and earthly. Thank you for your continued protection of my farm and my mother and sister. Help them, comfort them, hold them. Sustain them in this time of darkness, cover them in my absence. Thank you, Father God, thank you. Amen."

Joshua remained kneeling for a moment, lost in his prayer before placing his hand on his thigh and pushing up on the leg to raise himself off the ground. Placing his war cap upon his head, he adjusted the hair covering his eyes, wiping it behind his lobes. He tried to look across the field in front of him, but could see nothing. The sun was not fully out of its refuge.

In the air, there were small sounds of distant staccato musket fire. The silence of the battlefield caused his ears to ring. Sounds of just nature and a breeze running through the leaves of the gentle oaks and birch trees swelled in his ears. The rifle fire again sounded off in the early morning darkness.

His stomach had a nervous acid in it, bubbling and churning. He wanted no coffee, no food seemed to appease his mind. There was a stuffy, stymied presence lingering in the hot, humid atmosphere. He could not place his finger or his spirit on the problem. He just stared off into the darkness, into the subtle light beginning in front of his eyes.

The sun gradually rose across the field, across the horizon. Each minute of the morning, beams crossed east of his eyes. As if a blanket was slowly being lifted across the shin high grass, the sunlight caused a tide to form over the field. Soon there would be no darkness over the mile in front of Joshua's face.

Chapter Seventeen

The grass waved back and forth from the breeze, swaying from the breath of God. His eyes were transfixed upon the sight, lost in the abyss of this mind. Joshua's thoughts shifted from his farm to this field and then back again. His brain went chaotic inside his skull. Memories changing, going to and fro just as the grass.

Joshua's eyelids were drooping. The heat and chaotic thinking caused him to be complacent in his physical awareness. He was lost in thought, distracted by the scenery and silence. He didn't hear a soldier walk up and stand next to him. The soldier placed his back against the tree, bent his knee and lifted his right foot setting on the bark.

"You with us Josh?"

"Wha......oh, yes. I am here," he replied. "What can I do for you Nate?"

"Wonderin....just wonderin what the idea is. What the plan fer today is?"

"No clue, Nate. Nothing yet. Heard some rumors that we are going up right there," pointing his fingers across the field in front of them.

"That'd be stupid."

"Yeah. Other than the usual army gossip, I ain't heard nothin' as of yet."

"What if we do go across that field, Josh?"

"What about it? I reckon we go."

"Well, it just seems a bit crazy, sir. That is plenty of dirt to cover, a long way up. I surely do hope we heard wrong. There ain't gonna be one man who'll survive that march, sir."

"We step off whenever and wherever we are commanded Nate. Not at just the common sense battlefields. Remember two things, them Yankees are runners, have been since Mannassas. The second, we got God on our side. All we are asking for is no intrusion from the government. God don't like his people in bondage. Unlike the Israelites we didn't put ourselves in bondage."

"No. We just put others in it."

Joshua thought on what Nate had said. His brows scrunched together, the wrinkles on his forehead formed the thoughtful lines of concentration.

"You're right. I have lived my life by the principles of the Bible, and in one swift conjecture you have flipped my mind. I have always thought about the readings of the New Testament about slavery and minding your master. I guess that made me think slavery was...well...was God given. But then why would God put the Israelites into slavery to teach them? Nate, I have a great deal to ask God about."

"Then I will leave you to your prayers. I hope God tells you, I hope....I hope He gives you an answer to all our questions. What this is about and is it worth."

"I'll talk to you later Nate." With that he left Joshua standing by the tall oak, leaves fluttering in the ghostly humid breeze.

Standing for a moment near the tree, he then turned and began walking northward toward the seminary. He hoped a small morning stroll and prayer would clear his mind. A small war raged deep within Joshua's skull. He didn't notice if anyone saluted or said greetings of any kind. He walked in a fog, in a transfixed daze. Not even the heavy odor of food frying and coffee boiling brought him out of the stupor.

He didn't get far before he fell down to his knees in a secluded area. The trees around him formed a dense foliage barrier. Joshua hadn't noticed how deep in the woods he had walked, but it came to a twenty foot circular clearing. He could look above him and see the bright blue sky and a few hazy white clouds. He removed his kepi and put his face to the dirt patch below him. Joshua began to weep uncontrollably as his cause had been turned suddenly on its top.

Chapter Seventeen

"Father, my soul is exceedingly sorrowful, even unto death. What am I to believe God? What purpose is there to have in this battle? What am I to understand about what we are doing, Father in heaven?" Joshua cried out from the dirt. He lifted is face, tears descending down his cheeks, upper lip encrusted with dirt. He rolled onto his back and raised his hands to the heavens.

Joshua lay there, eyes closed, the light going in and out of focus as the clouds passed over the sun above. No words formed out of his mouth, no vocalization seemed to resonate from this throat. His chest raised gradually, then blew out rapidly as a wind storm out of the calm. He continued to breath in this form of absolute urgency, his convictions and beliefs hanging on each inhalation.

His eyes dashed open in a frenzy of welcoming light, his retinas dilating as he pushed his body off the ground. "Of course, God!" he yelled, "Thank you, thank you!" Joshua wept tears of joy and gladness as he did an about face and walked the way in which he came.

His feet moved with both swiftness and care as he retraced his steps back to his company. One foot would lead in front of the other, stepping over fallen branches of the wooded area, twigs snapping and cracking under the weight of his body. Old dead leaves crinkled and crushed from his black boots. His hands waved out in front of him, chopping the brush away from his face. The upper torso bobbed back and forth to the left and right as his body moved through the foliage. All the way he spat out praises and thanks to God, while he spat out leaves and bugs that invaded his mouth as he ran.

He reached the road on Seminary ridge and saw the heavy movement of the Southern army fantastically coordinating maneuvers. Cannons were being wheeled behind horses, caissons rattling their armaments, the tinkling and clinking of metal swords and brass buckles could be heard. The sound of weighted hooves stomped the ground and squeaky wagon wheels pitched through the trees. Joshua stood there, his head turning to the left and to the right watching and listening, awe struck at the visionary splendor of the sight.

The cannons turned left into a field as Joshua continued on this way back to his company. The running strides and movements of his body ceased as he now walked towards his destination, not wanting to have worrisome eyes cast upon him. The excitement that was in the air created enough of a panic stricken atmosphere now to have a rushing lieutenant add to the circumstances.

Vast amounts of men lay in the shade of the trees, attempting to find refuge from the ghastly heat. Their unbuttoned jackets rested upon their shoulders allowing some air to breathe through them, but the sweat soaked shirts they wore gave a different expression and smell. The shirts revealed the frailty of the day, the one weakness neither army could combat, the muggy, humid, putrid hot air that permeated through the oxygen. The mixture of heat and war caused men to be weary and trigger fingers to be burdensome on the hand.

One man caught Joshua's eyes, a sight that made his heart rejoice, yet be saddened. With the Southerner's single leg, he hobbled around on his crutches but stayed with his unit. The terrain made it difficult for the crippled man and the left crutch bowed in the middle causing a noticeable limp as he walked. But the man stayed true to his comrades, his brothers in arms.

His eyes locked on this man and caused Joshua to stop walking. The confirmation of God's message had been sent, the reason for his cause strained to simply walk among his brothers. The reason for his cause filled his retinas and put his tear ducts to action. The reason for his cause had been around him the entire time.

Chapter Seventeen

Turning from the scene, his feet took him back to his tree overlooking the field. A grumbling rose about the noise of the day. Distant muskets firing off, a few thunderous cannons, birds chirping, leaves blowing and the sound of the Army of Northern Virginia moving. The grumbling sounded again and realizing it was his own stomach, Joshua acknowledged his hunger.

He reached inside his tunic, pulling out a biscuit and bit into it. The stale flour tasting nutrition entered his mouth as he chewed repeatedly. Swinging his canteen around from his side, he took a swig. The water swished around in his mouth before slowly exiting down his throat. Joshua repeated this sequence until his food was gone, all the time his eyes remaining upon the open field.

A cracking twig made his head turn to the left and there was Nate, also looking across the field. "I think we heard right about going across. That's the biggest rumor around, still hoping it ain't true."

"Well, we sure will find out soon. If we are to take those heights, we will need plenty of time and men."

"Did you pray? Not trying to pry..."

"That's fine. I did pray and I did hear."

"What did you hear?"

"Plenty. An earful. I did not know where to start while praying. I was at a loss for words, all I could do was cry, thinking that we put so many people in bondage. I sobbed outta desperation hoping to hear, just wanting an answer. I heard Zechariah 7:10, so I pulled out my small Bible from the breast pocket of my jacket and looked it up.

"It says, *And oppress not the widow, not the fatherless, the stranger, not the poor; and let none of you imagine evil against his brother in your heart.* You see, I could not fight against my fellow brother, my neighbors, while the Yankees continued to tell us what to do with our land. While coming back I saw a lame man walking on bowed crutch, staying with his friends. That is when I saw what God was trying to show me. Some may fight for the slaves, but I do not nor do many from the South. We are fighting for the right to govern ourselves, much as we did in our independence war."

For a while the two men discussed this, sharing Bible verses and their opinions of each verse. In the midst of their discussion Colonel Fry approached and called the two men to the regimental meeting. They rose and followed their commander to a circle of men standing around a desk outside a tent. Smoke from cigars and pipes fogged through the air, becoming stagnant with the residue of campfire smoke and humid air. The fog that ensued lingered just above their heads, circling amongst the trees.

"Gentlemen, this has just come down from General Longstreet and the commanders at the top. Our objective is to....well, it is to cross that open field." said Fry, the other men looking at each other. "We will be positioned with the rest of the division, as well as the whole corp. General Heth was wounded, we all know that. General Pettigrew will be in command for this attack.

"You see, the center is weak. The flanks have been reinforced through the night as well as good artillery backing them up. General Lee has the information that the center is the weakest point on the battlefield. Our artillery will lead our stepping off point, they will precede us with firing on the center, driving their guns off the field. After that, we will march up and break their line in two. General Early and his men will attack their right flank and at the same time causing mass confusion for the Yanks."

"Sir? Where do we march to?"

"There is a clump of trees in the center, look across the field and you can see them. That is the objective. Gentleman, this could end the war. By nightfall, we could be free from the tyranny of Lincoln and his folly."

Chapter Seventeen

None of the officers cheered or whooped. They smirked and smiled, mentally preparing for the attack. Fry dismissed them, returning them to their men.

Joshua's haste filled steps carried him back to his awaiting sergeant. "Gather the men, I need to give the company their instructions." The sergeant turned and left as Johsua rubbed his hands together due to the nervous tension in the air.

As the men filed into their places, surrounding the young lieutenant, the excitement and curiosity caused them to talk incessantly, vocalizing every thought. Soon the deafening conversation filled circle enveloped the area.

"Quiet! Quiet down men!" yelled Joshua as they slowly complied. He discussed and directed the orders that had been given. Describing each company's mission and what their objective was, at the end he paused and began to speak again. "We will form up in these trees. Be in position men, be ready to step off, there will be no time to reposition once on that field. Know this....you are my brothers, you are my neighbors. Our command is to love our neighbors and I love each of you.

"You are fine men and fine soldiers and great brothers. This siege we have been through for so many years is to end. We are to have our freedom today. We are to have our victory today. Let us not fear the outcome of ...of well anything that might happen this day."

He reached into his tunic and pulled out his Bible. The pages crackled and shook in his hand. "But whoso hearkeneth unto me shall dwell safely, and shall be quiet from fear of evil." Proverbs 1:33. Seek God and listen and he will drive fear from you and instill it into your enemies. Form up!" Joshua crescendoed from a whisper to a war cry.

The men screamed and yelled back moving to the tree line in front of the field. Platoon commanders instructed their men where to place themselves, completed ammunition checks along the way down their lines. The afternoon sun beat down through the trees and added to the heat of the commotion and trepidation.

Scurrying men ended their futile fidgeting while commanders stayed their voices. As the movements ended, artillery opened their barrage of God like thunder, raining the chaos down upon the enemy. The men became deathly silent as the realism of war set in. They listened to the echo ringing tones of the cannons. Anderson looked down at this gold pocket watch. Two o'clock pm.

Each artillery man had a duty and as such they worked in harmony with each other. Their movement precise and actions deadly. When the cannon was fired, each man on the team had a job to perform. Six men plus an officer working together as brother. All striving for the same objective, driving the enemy off their ridge.

Singularly each cannon fired, shooting out its ball of destruction. The gases would ignite exploding in the barrel and send its projectile toward the objective. The third team member rushed forward, placing his left hand over a vent, closing off the oxygen supply. The first member used a long sponge staff and cleared the barrel awaiting artilleryman number two to insert the round into the muzzle. He would then turn the staff around and plunge the projectile down into the barrel.

The gunner aimed the cannon, setting it back into place after it rolled back from the recoil. "Ready!" he yelled out. Artillery men one, two and three set themselves in the ready position. The fourth man inserted the primer and fired the cannon. Each time this occurred, each movement was exact, every man having a job. Every thirty seconds the cannons were ready.

Joshua's men sat, kneeled or stood during the duration of the artillery barrage. Each side firing at the other. Explosions causing ears to go numb and heads began to ache. The noise

Chapter Seventeen

was of such a volume, the men had to cover their ears or stuff bits of cloth into them to keep them from hurting.

Each time a cannon fired it seemed as though the enemy had a response. A question and an answer in, what felt like, a debate of destruction, an argument of arbitration. Hopes were held high as heads were held low, trying to avoid the sounds. Closed eyes caused memories to flash and anxiety to levitate to the forefront of each mind. No words could be spoken, no words wanted to be spoken.

An eternity of ear bleeding noise gradually came to an end. The word had been passed down through the ranks to form up. Joshua gathered his company outside the tree line and moved into the shin high grass. The company, regiment all the way up to the division and whole corp assembled and joined marching ranks.

Joshua looked down the line moving his head from one side to the other, his eyes were filled with the color of gray and butternut. The flags of states, regiments and of the Confederacy blew rapidly in the wind. The line stretched further than his vision could take him, the winding hill ending his line of sight.

Some one had given the order to fix bayonets and Joshua forwarded the order by yelling out to his company and beyond, "Bayonets!" The clinking of steel on tin and metal pitched high in the humidity. Down the line and over the hills the sound could be heard as a wave, each man attaching the steel body piercing tool of death. The order came to march and Joshua complied and barked out the order.

Drums began to beat and feet began to move, boots, wrapped feet and bare feet marched along the grass. As the drummers swung their sticks and flutes played their tune, Lieutenant Joshua Anderson and his men faithfully stepped off.

Chapter Eighteen

◆

Lamentations 3:38

Is it not from the mouth of the most high that both calamities and good things come?

July 3, 1863

The leather moaned as James Spalding pulled on the strap. Metal jingled as he buckled the girth to the billet straps. He placed two fingers between the straps and the horse's body, slapping the saddle making sure it was secure and not too tight.

James rubbed his temples with his middle fingers trying to alleviate the pain in his head. The pounding of his heart pumped blood into the vessels of his brain, the absence of alcohol caused it to hurt. The eyelids on his face closed from slight into extreme darkness. Every muscle was stiff from riding, his face still deeply bruised from a rifle stock and now his head beat ferociously like a bass drum.

After sharing about Matt's death, everyone in the camp tried to comfort James, but all was futile. The attempts fell upon deaf ears and a hardened heart. He would simply not

Chapter Eighteen

listen to reason and reality, but chose to become bitter and bewitched by hatred.

The early morning hours brought some sun and more heat to the battlefield. A corporal with an unbuttoned jacket and suspenders hanging out the back approached James as he rubbed his horse's nose.

"Goin' for a ride, Captain?"

"It *is* my horse, Corporal."

"Want some company?"

"I am just going to check on the different companies, get a feel of morale. If you choose to join me go ahead, pretty sure I will not be good company, thought."

"I could tag along I guess."

"Suit yourself," replied James putting his foot in the left stirrup and pulling himself up by the mane. With a kick from his right heal the horse moved forward.

"You alright, sir?"

"I don't feel much like talking. Been a bad couple days."

"All we can do is pray for help."

"Pray to whom, God? If he *is* real then he just lets people die."

"Is that what you truly believe Captain? Because that would go against all that has been taught to us," replied the corporal.

"That is what I believe now."

"I guess I did not know that you were feeling sorry for yourself.".

"I do not need a lecture from a corporal."

"Sir, no disrespect, I am appalled."

"I get it! I am sorry, but I just cannot get this whole thing into perspective right now. The God I was so determined to serve and love..the God I worshiped has let me down," James said angrily.

"Do you even hear yourself, Captain? Right now all I hear is 'me, me, I, I' from you. It is quite selfish."

"What would you have me say? Praise God?"

"How about *that is war* or even *it's just life*?"

"Do not believe that statement."

"How about *it is the work of the devil?*"

"His Word lied to me. Everything I learned and believed just lied to me!"

"Perhaps you lied to the Word or better yet God."

"What do you mean?" asked James, pulling his reins to stop the horse. They sat atop their mounts underneath the shade of a tall pine tree.

"I heard that in Isaiah it says 'my word be that goeth out of my mouth: it shall not return unto me void'".

"Yes....alright, but what does that....." James mumbled.

"Just because it does not return to God void does not mean that it does not return to you void. You did not believe fully as God does." James stared at the sap he noticed oozing from the pine and listened. "I was also taught about Christ and the things he did. What I found on my own reading is that there was a moment when Jesus could not heal someone because of their faith. Because they had none."

"But I did," James whispered, staring off into the distance.

"Faith that what? That no man shall die in war or peace. That is not something you put your faith in. I apologize for the rudeness, sir. I must leave. I have business to get to."

The two men exchanged looks, nodded and went their separate ways. James stayed a minute longer, his brain processing all that was said. With a swift kick from his leg and a poke from his heel, the horse lurched forward. He rode into various companies from different brigades, mingling with the men.

The stories were different in names, but the same in style. The love of home and family and the hatred of the distance between them. The men came from all sorts of backgrounds and from the upper east coast to the Midwest.

Chapter Eighteen

Maine to Minnesota, Maryland to Michigan, the men hailed their home states, each better than the other. Some had a sense of duty to give to their blessed Union, others were roped in by the government. Complaints were boisterously held high as swords drawn from a sheath and praises given in heartfelt confessions. A weariness ran through the muscles and veins and a leeriness ran through the brains and thought patterns. Some wanted to run, some to just walk away, but the over-all reason each man stuck to his post was due to the one next to him.

He turned the reins, moving towards a generals' headquarters. The horse clopped along, her hooves stomping the ground below. James spoke to the mare in a soothing tone, perhaps to pass the time, perchance to talk to someone. The horse carried him to his destination as he rode in a daze. The leather creaked and moaned at him as he swayed back and forth in the saddle.

In the distance he saw a general pacing back and forth, smoke puffing on his pipe. The anxiousness from his walking to and fro caused men to stir and a colonel to motion him to sit down, but his pacing continued.

Dismounting the horse, James walked up to the two men. "Please tell the General to stop being so anxious. It only hurts the men," said the colonel.

Looking at both, James was confused by the actions of the two men.

"I cannot help it. I hate sitting still. I like to be on the move. Have been since childhood," replied General Merritt. "I need you to take two companies to General Custer. He is at the east of us."

The sweltering heat made him feel languid in the saddle. As he looked around he saw the soldiers of his brigade lazily moving around in the late morning. Once again he began to think to himself about the meaning of this fight, about the reason for all this death and carnage.

What purpose does all this serve? A day ago all things seemed to be clear to me. God, if You are out there, what purpose is this for? My goodness, they're cutting legs off in front of everybody, stacking arms up like kindling. At one time I thought we were an army to liberate but now I wonder if the Negroes are truly worth it. Is all this death truly worth freeing a race of man? Of course, we wanted to be free at one time. Free from the abuses and usurpations of a foreign government and many men died then as well.

This country was founded upon blood, this flag is stained with blood. Where do we go from this day or the next day? Where do we go from this war? Freedom? What a word. Some men dream of the true meaning as others spew their blood for the definition.

A small breeze picked up from the south but caused no alleviation from the heat, only bringing the putrid smell of decaying flesh. The heat and wild boars processed the dead to ghastly smells and unrecognizable features. The cries of wounded fell upon the deaf ears of nature; no one being able to help.

He looked down from his horse and saw a dead soldier lying in a ditch. He had been drug there by a comrade, his mouth draped open, eyes with a bewildered glaze looked up at James. He knew not his name nor his unit, but James knew him by his story. He donned the uniform of his country, ran to live for his brother, died in battle for the freedom of an entire race. His family might receive word from a letter or a name in the newspaper, but comfort would not come to their hearts. The solemn promise that he made to come home, now broken, would make it hard to push through the tears of stately shock, denial and hatred.

Thousands of families would be going through the emotions of death. Fathers would not shake their son's hands, mothers would not hug again and children would not sit on the knee and have stories of teaching and love. Handkerchiefs

Chapter Eighteen

will be washed in tears and thrown out from fear, for no one could know the pain and anguish of their suffering.

James kicked his horse and continued back to his company. He rode down a path, grass trampled down by wagons and hooves. The dirt kicked up by feet and boots, a road not made by gravel and not put on any map. The terrain was rocky, a happenstance of the mountains surrounding the small Pennsylvania town. It made for difficult journeys and maneuvers fraught with trepidation as a man sat in a saddle strapped to a thousand pound animal.

The brown and white sorrel cautiously found her footing while moving into a dried up brook gorge that led back to James' company of calvary. He leaned back in the saddle putting pressure on her hind legs to give more support and relieve the immobility of weight on her front legs. She stopped at the bottom and began to relieve herself. Jim stood up in the stirrups to alleviate the pressure of his body on her kidneys. Once she was finished, they made the climb up the other side of the embankment, her hooves clomped on the stone and skidded a little bit. They made their way to the top without alarm.

The camp was bustling with activity, some men sat around awaiting orders, their poker cards clicking together as they shuffled. The middle of camp played the music of a fiddle and guitar to the tune of "We Are Coming, Father Abraham, Three Hundred Thousand More." Some men laid lounging, propped up on elbows reading letters, others shaded their eyes with books as they napped on the grass.

James stopped his horse, drawing her to a halt, then swinging his right leg over her hind haunches he slowly let it down to the ground. He finished dismounting the mare and used a quick release knot to tie her to a low level branch. Removing his hat from his head and smoothing out his long blond hair, he entered his tent and sat down at a desk.

Pulling a piece of parchment paper from a slotted portion of the storage space, he began to write a letter. His pencil tapped against the paper while his left hand lifted towards his face. The thumb of his hand rubbed the left side of his mustache, the fingers the other side, while his palm brushed his lips and chin hair. His blue eyes glazed, pupils dilating as he thought on the days behind him and those in front.

The writing instrument sat upon the paper, the two becoming one with words. The letter was dated to his daughter and how he wished he could have known her and how much she truly meant to him even though they had never met. Jim wrote on how he did not need a picture of her but only knew how she looked and how absolutely beautiful she was.

"Sir, platoon leaders are gathered and awaiting instructions," burst in a young sergeant.

"Thank you. I will be out in a moment." replied James while lifting himself out of the chair and putting the letter in his breast pocket. He pushed the flap open and stepped into the sunlight that broke through the thick green leaves. The platoon leaders were gathered around in a circle, one man threw a peach to the captain.

"Men found a peach tree. Thought we would save one for you."

"Thank you Lieutenant," replied James taking a bite. The juice ran down his chin catching in his facial hair. He wiped it on his sleeve. Pink and yellow and a little crispy, it crunched in his mouth as he chewed. Swallowing, he began to speak. "Gentlemen, this heat and humidity is blazing hell out here. No matter what we do this day, keep your men and yourselves with water. Many a man will fall out due to heat.

"Secondly, I have been instructed per General Merritt to deliver you to General Custer to the east of the center. I guess there is a mass of cavalry there, and we are to concentrate."

"What happens if they attack the center?"

Chapter Eighteen

"As highly unlikely as that is, we will have to see. If need be, we will dismount and join them in the fight. I do not see anything like that happening though," replied James. "Get to it gentleman, it is a simple day."

The men adjourned off to their respective companies and James pulled a cigar out from the inside of his upper left breast pocket as he entered his tent. He bit off a small piece of the end and spit it out on the grass. Striking a match on the heel of his boot, he lit the cigar and sucked in the sweet tasting smoke and blew it out into the air. He sat down in a wooden folding chair awaiting the platoon leaders to report they were in position to move out.

The heat and humidity caused him to wipe his forehead with a handkerchief, once pure white now stained with dirt and dust as well as blood and sweat. Captain Spalding perspired profusely as the temperature reached triple digits along with the humidity. The heat may have caused him to sweat but his heavy heart caused him to daze off into his thoughts.

What do I tell his wife? How do I explain that I could not help him? Her heartache is to be most intense, overwhelming. What words can comfort and explain the situation at the same time? How do I tell her that her husband died from a freak accident of his horse throwing him off? If I have all these questions, how much many will she have and how will I answer them if I cannot even answer my own?

The silence became deafening to James, though the sounds of battle could be heard in the distance and the movement of all the hooves on sod pummeled along. His ears rang out from the silence of his deep transient thoughts, his brain actively moving about the subject. The anxiousness of the day could not be felt by James at the moment. A numbness came upon his body as he remained motionless and limp in his chair. The right shoulder acted as a rest for the head of the body while his hands dangled off to the side, cigar smoke slowly rising from the un-smoked cigar.

The young sergeant came back and entered the tent. He removed his kepi to reveal his ruffled wavy black hair, as he scratched his left side burn that extended down to his jawline. The mustache he attempted to grow was beginning to show the absence of shaving, his pursuit to look older. The green eyes that inhabited his face gazed at his captain. "Sir, the company is formed and ready to move."

James turned his head slowly, gradually coming out of his trance. "What is the time Sergeant?"

The sergeant scrunched his brow together, wondering why his captain did not look at his own watch, but merely pulled out his pocket watch. "It is one-thirty, sir." he replied clicking the face cover closed while replacing the timepiece back into its dark resting place in his pocket.

"Right. Then mount your ride and let us get moving on."

"Yes, sir," he replied, his tooth filled grin revealing his excitement.

James exited his tent, closing the flap behind him and donned his flat, slightly crowned blue hat that held on it the U.S. Insignia encircled by leaves. Climbing aboard his mare after he had released the knot, he pulled back and to the left, turning her around. With a kick of his heels she darted to the front of his company and coming forth from cigar filled mouth, he gave the order to move out.

In columns of two they rode northeast of their camp to meet up with the trains of supplies coming in. The horses moved at a slow trot, not quite a walk but not in a full trotting stride. James rode alongside his second in command, the commander of first platoon, while puffing on his cigar. His stained gloves held onto the reins as his body slightly bobbed up and down from the trotting horse.

The two men rode in silence, hearing only the sounds of heavy hooves on gravel dirt and squeaking leather on

Chapter Eighteen

tired backsides. Their swords struck their legs, clinking and clanging as they rode on to their destination. The scenery enveloped their eyes, the masses of men marching or those encamped and sitting around as they passed by. Some hobbled on a crutch, others walked without an arm and still some were in perfect health.

The shade brought comfort to none with the amount of bodies that piled under them. Many lay strewn about attempting some relief from the heat, but could find nothing of the sort. The green hues and pigments of what was a beautiful landscape two days ago was now the sight of much carnage. Entangled corpses and mangled bodies scattered the outside of hospitals, while men lined them up in shallow ditches.

James refused to yield to the sight and remained focused on the path in front of him. The road was straight, small hills causing it to rise and fall while they made their mission of relief and supplementation. Spitting out the stub of his cigar, he spoke for the first time. "Up ahead is the split in the road, Lieutenant. Ride to the depot and supply your men with what they need for ammunition and weapons. We will then proceed to the artillery batteries in the center."

The lieutenant responded his understanding and moved his company down the right split. Spalding instructed his men to form a defensive triangle covering the intersection. With General Stuart on the prowl James wanted no surprises to pick apart the companies. Being behind their lines and with the ability of Stuart to ride around the entirety of the army did nothing to help James but only made him more nervous. His company sat out in the open.

As he sat atop his mount he overheard two enlisted men with shoulders turned away talking in hoarse voices, in an obvious attempt not to be overheard.

"He's different, you know, actin' wise," the first whispered.

"He ain't all that different, just quiet. You'd be too if'n you saw your brother-in-law die," the other replied softly.

"I seen many men die in this here war. Sure it changes you, but he seen men die too. Why now he got a problem?"

"Don't know, I guess it was too much."

"Hope he holds up. Nerves can be a swelterin' thing."

James dismounted his horse and walked over to the two men. Upon hearing the footsteps, they turned and their eyes grew wide and their mouth shut up tight as they saw him there. "Private Lewis," James said looking at one. "Private Helterline," he nodded to the other. "Are you men alright?"

"Yes, sir," replied Lewis.

"Yes, sir. Just ready to move out," said Helterline.

"Well...you are two good men. Ride careful and do not let your nerves get the best of you." said Spalding looking at each in the eye.

"Yes, Sir," they replied in unison. James walked down the line, a small smirk on his face and checked on his other men before returning to his mare and climbing aboard her.

A half hour passed by and there was no sign of first platoon returning back to the split in the road. Checking his watch several times, James was beginning to pace his horse up and down the lines. "I should have gone with them," he muttered to himself.

"You cannot go with everybody and be with everyone, sir," said a lieutenant. "We needed you here, with most of the men."

"I know. I just do not like it," replied James. "They should have been back by now. It concerns me." Just as he finished his sentence the sound of wagons and horses could be heard down the road. "Hold steady boys. We do not know who that is as of yet."

They could see the dust of the road rising up into the air, but no sign of who the troops were. The threat of enemy movement caused James' hand to reach down to his black

Chapter Eighteen

leather holster containing his pistol. He slowly and cautiously unsnapped the gold peg and lightly brushed his fingertips over the butt end of the pistol.

A hill prevented them from seeing any lead element in front of them. A horse's nose rose above the crest, Jim palmed the revolver on his right hip. He then saw the face of his lieutenant, relaxed his hand and snapped the holster back in place.

"Sorry sir, we were held up by the supply trains being a little behind schedule."

"Fine. Let us get moving!" he yelled.

The horses thundered along at a full gallop, drudging down the road. Their movements were mechanically precise, their stride elegantly designed. The muscles tightened and loosened while the legs extended and retracted moving to their destination. Cannon fire could be heard in the short distance, getting louder and more boisterous as the cavalry enclosed.

Showers of dirt were raining down upon the earth when James reached his destination. The world seemed to slow down and all noise happened to allude his ears as he watched the cannons fire. The thoughts of his friend streamed by his mind as a river rushed after a heavy rain. He saw an older major yelling at him, but could not hear the man.

"I said thank God you are here. We have been firing hot since about three!"

"That is fine and all but I do not have the supplies you are looking for. I am only trying to find a certain outfit. You guys are completely out of ammunition?" asked Jim.

"Just ran out a little while ago. Since you guys are not the ones who will deliver our ammunition who will be?" asked the artillery officer.

"I wish I could answer that for you but I cannot. I can only hope with you sir." The man cursed a little wishing for better news.

Upon The Eastern Sun

The world came screaming back to Captain James Spalding. A squealing shell came hurling down towards the two men talking and exploded into an empty caisson parked nearby. The splinters and wood flew through the air causing a shower of slivers and a down pour of shrapnel to fall on them. A piece ripped through the pants of Spalding causing him to immediately clutch his leg and his horse to rear up. His other hand slipped from the grip of the rein, his backside falling out of the saddle. Upon his landing on the ground he looked at his hand, his leather stained glove now painted with red.

Chapter Nineteen

Psalm 119:106

I have sworn and I will perform it.

July 3, 1863

"I do not care for it! Not one bit! I know I agreed to stay, but I was a topographical engineer before the war. I know the use of ground and the advantages it can have," sputtered Meade.

"Yes, sir. General Hancock seems to...."

"Hancock is a good officer, sometimes he can be a bit aggressive. At times we must be more reserved, more passive in our movements," interrupted the general.

"It seems that is what we have had in the past. We might want something new, sir."

"Major, how long have you been in the army?"

"Several years, sir," replied the major standing from his seat and moving toward the window. "Sun is coming up sir. Another day. Hopefully it can be the last."

"I wish it could be. Unfortunately war never seems to work within a man's schedule. They always come at inopportune times and always draw confusion," said Meade.

"Well, sir, it is not always about the time as it is the interruption of life and of course the carnage," replied the major sipping his hot coffee from his tin cup continuing to look out the window at the sunrise.

"I am not new to war Major...." the General's statement was imposed upon the sounds of bustle on the right of the line. "Do we know what that is about Major?"

"Sir, General Geary returned during the night and it was mentioned that he was going to retake the ground on the right that was lost yesterday. I do believe that is what we are hearing."

"Yes, I know. Geary and most of twelfth corps was sent to reinforce the left. Apparently he has returned to the right."

"Yes, sir. "

"Good, it seems the enemy will have no choice but to attack the flanks again," said Meade.

"How is that sir?"

"With them taking ground and also not getting ground they believe our flanks are weak. They will attack thinking that we are weakened, not knowing we have reinforced the flanks and are strong."

"Yes, sir."

"What I mean by that is on the right they pushed our troops but on the left we held strong. They will be empowered by pushing us and upset by not pushing us on the left. They want the flanks."

Yes, sir. But what about our center?"

"Too risky. Even at their estimated strength of over one hundred thousand. That gray old fox is smarter than that, more cunning. Anyway, I am sorry to have kept you up all night."

"Not at all, Sir. I do not mind."

"We will soon have reports streaming in. Let us get ready for it."

****

The match shimmered in the darkness, the flame dancing in the breeze. Extending the match to the pipe, Buford sucked in the smoky tobacco and held it in his mouth before releasing the cloud of smoke. He paced the ground continuously, his feet being heavily placed one in front of the other. The trains at Westminster had him somewhat bored, while he sent his other officers out to protect the wagons.

The early morning sun brought late day heat, but early risers reported in. They were eager, at least some of them, even after the exploits two days prior. Their boyish grins and snap salutes showed exuberance of their youth and shattered values of life they once knew. Buford scratched his mustache and shook his head. "Boys. But my boys."

"What was that, sir?"

Buford turned to see Colonel Devin standing there holding a coffee cup in one hand, the other held his kept as he wiped his forehead with his sleeve. "Oh, nothing. Just thinking out loud."

"I see. Do it all the time, General," he replied setting the cup of coffee in front of Buford.

"Good to know, Devin."

Colonel Devin sat down, accepting a cup of coffee for himself from an aide. "Seems them Rebs are fit to fight sir."

"It does seem that way."

"I believe the fate of our country rests on this battle, sir. I believe all could be lost if we lose."

"Said that two days ago. Nothing has changed in my mind still."

"There is a different sense about this battle though, a.....a feeling of redemption for us."

"How so?" Buford looked questioningly at the man.

"Well, it feels as though there is a drive. A want for victory. Not like Fredricksburg where the men marched up the bloody heights out of a numbness to orders. Or Chandellorville where we ran scared. We want this. We need this!"

"I agree with the needing this victory, but as for feeling it....well, I'm too tired and worn for those feelings. Sometimes I feel like riding off to Rock Island and seeing Pattie, but then I think about these boys and this country. As much as I miss my wife, I would miss the feeling of love for this nation. That is the only feeling I have had of late." A horse whinnied and Buford turned, "What's the problem Eagle?" Buford turned back to Devin.

"Even Grey Eagle wants to get riding, sir," said Devin.

"Seems that way."

"I know we are all eager to get back in the saddle, but we need more men."

"I am just happy to not be riding a desk job, but to be out in the field. I thought I would go crazy having to hear about the troops and not be with them."

"I can understand that, sir. I have been awaiting orders."

"We'll be staying in Westminster today. Guard the supply trains. Sun is just over the east right now. I'll have more later."

"Yes, sir. I will return then or if you want, you could send for me."

"Very well Colonel." With that Devin left the general alone.

****

In a different room, boots heavily thumped along the wooden floors and smoke fogged the air. Reports speedily rolled off tongues. Meade clicked the button on his watch and read the face at 12:45 pm. He looked up at the middle aged Lieutenant Colonel giving his report about the action

Chapter Nineteen

of his regiment at Devil's Den, his eyes half open, ears half listening.

"We were pushed back, General. Fought on those rocks like hell, sir. Lost most of my boys, I'm down to about a quarter strength in my regiment."

"Thank you for your report. Take your men to the rear and rest. Do not go far, your services still may be required."

"Yes, General."

"Is there anybody else who is important enough to have to see me Major?" asked Meade once the Lieutenant Colonel had left.

"No one at this time General."

"Very well. It is fifteen to one Major. Other than the action this morning on the right, it has been a fairly quiet day thus far. Too hot for the enemy and truth be told...too muggy for me as well."

"General, more supply requests have come in. General Sykes has made a request, *Ammunition shortage drastic. Battle at Little Round Top ended with bayonet charge. Need supplies. Most urgent.* That is the same requests we have coming in all the time."

"I have Buford's men down in Westminster to protect supply trains. Have Sykes pull some of his men off those hills, bring them to the center. They can get a hot meal and some much needed rest."

"Yes, General."

"Oh, and Major."

"Yes?"

"Commend them for holding the line."

"Yes, General."

General Meade stood up from his desk and walked to the window watching the stirring of men outside. Legs moved with swiftness in some of their steps, while others leaned against the fence posts in the yard. Some men dabbed their foreheads with a cloth and others wiped the sweat with their sleeves, but the most common action taking place was a trifling shuffle of men attempting to stay conscious from the heat.

Out of the calm of the day, a shattering explosion came from the right of the house. Meade turned his head sharply and saw shards of wood flying through the air. His eyes lifted to the sky and saw cannonballs raining down on his headquarters. The world seemed to slow down and everyone's behavior moved second by second. The calm shuffles that had once been were no more as men jumped into covered positions while the dirt showered down upon their heads. A blast outside the window caused General Meade to dive onto the floor, the glass of panes breaking trickled down on him. The Major kicked open the front door and ran to Meade.

"General! The Rebs have opened up a whole world of cannons!" the major screamed. "We need to get you out of here!"

"No! I must stay in command!"

"Sir you won't have much of a command when you are dead."

"Fine. Hancock's in charge."

They ran out the door and to the saddled horses, which were prancing around nervously. The world opened up and splinters and dirt once more pitched down upon them.

****

"What do you wish to do with the enemy's dead, General?"

"Enemy?"

"Yes, sir. Looks like some of Stuart's men may have come into the hands of militia."

"Line them up for burial. Even the enemy deserves a proper burial. They are still our countrymen," replied Buford.

"Yes, General," retorted the trooper.

Chapter Nineteen

"We have seen too much," said Buford quietly under his breath.

He rode atop his mount directing Colonels Gamble and Devin where to place their brigades in exact symmetry with the supply train. He wanted nothing left to chance. He knew that Stuart's cavalry had already been here before the battle, as could be seen by a few of the dead Confederates lying in ditches.

"Colonel Gamble!" yelled Buford.

Gamble trotted his horse next to the General's. "Yes, General?"

"Any news about Captain Spalding?"

Gamble shook his head.

"We left him to that?" hearing massive cannon fire.

"Yes, sir."

"Very well." Buford looked at his gold watch, reading the hands at ten after one. In the distance he could hear thunder rising. Gamble was saying something about the beauty of the mass movement of soldiers. "Hold on Colonel."

Buford's eyes squinted, brows burrowing into his face, listening intently. "Sounds like plenty of cannon fire."

Gamble took a moment to listen. "Yes General, that sure does sound like a world full of artillery." He wiped his eyes with his sleeves.

"It's coming from Gettysburg. We just left Spalding in a hell storm!"

"He should be alright General. The boy knows how to take care of himself."

The General remained silent, lost in reverie, listening to the intense artillery duel taking place in Gettysburg. He scratched his mustache, then removed his hat and smoothed his hair from left to right. Donning his hat upon his head, his eyes fixated over the horizon to the north. Lost in his thoughts, he caused his men to be addle in his mind.

The train's engine blew off steam from the smoke stack, whistle blowing loudly. The box car's doors slid open, men placing ramps onto the decks, and supplies began to lurch down the wooden planks. Barrels rolled on their sides, wagons squeaked and creaked down the slope. Men yelled out to each other, asking for assistance, where they were from, what was happening on the line. None of the noise broke Buford's stare.

He finally broke his silence, turning to Gamble. "How to take care of himself? Yes that is true. I am afraid all that he has done over the past days might be lost. I am afraid that all we have done is ordered that boy to his end. All we have done is left him into the devil's lair. He's not coming out of that."

****

The fire cracked and crepitated as it spoke its soothing voice to General Heth. He had only slept for a couple hours in his rocking chair, hoping that his head would stop spinning, wishing that the pain would subside. No word from Pettigrew about the fighting and now he was awake, staring at the fire. The plan was thought out, it was complete, all that remained was execution. Now he was allowing doubt to creep into his mind during this precocious time of day.

Heth needed the troops to rise, to give him a feel of their energy. He was in exigence to know how the men felt after the previous day of battle. The Little Rocky Hill had been a drawback that he could not get back. Hood had lost most of his men and his arm. Heth couldn't afford to lose Pettigrew or any of his generals. The General felt as though he was sinking in his thoughts, he returned his gaze to the fire.

His brain turned back to the day ahead of him, focusing on the wall across the field. The men had to breach the wall, had to break their line. Without it, two days of fighting was

Chapter Nineteen

for naught. The death of thousands for nothing. Heth lifted himself out of the chair and walked over to the desk, boots pounding on the hard boards below him.

The map stared back at him, emotionless, not moving an inch. Artillery. That was the only thought Heth had on his mind. Artillery. They would have to push the enemy off the ridge they sat on. They would possess the task of breaking the Union core, softening their core for the infantry to march into Rome!

He turned from the map and strode over to the window watching the sun in its genesis stage of awakening life. That part of day where night still commands the land but an eerie purple haze can be seen in the east, steadily beating back the tenebrous sky. Heth nodded his head up and down as if answering his own question. Turning to a rack holding his tunic, he took it off the wooden stand and slipped on the coat. Slowly buttoning it up, he rubbed his forefinger over the insignia on the brass.

The knob on the door turned and the hinges squeaked while the entrance was opened. Heth stopped outside making his way to his horse, hoping to get him saddled and moving. The attendant who slept in the room next to the horses, awakened at the sound of Heth coming.

"I'll git him ready right quick, General."

"Good morning."

"Good mornin', General. You want to get out?"

"Yes, thank you." Heth stumbled a little, his head spinning the ground underneath him becoming unfocussed within his vision. He leaned on a tree, supporting his weight on the strong sturdy bark.

"Maybe we shouldn't sir."

****

Pettigrew's eyes dashed open, his breathing rushing heavily, chest rising and falling. Dreams had broken his sleep, the war shattering the slumber. He hadn't even realized he had fallen asleep until he woke up so suddenly. Standing to his feet the world slowly spun around him, while he twisted his neck to work out the stiff pertinacious muscles.

The flap of his tent opened with a push of his hand. Crickets sounded off in the early dawn announcing their role call. Embers of the fire lay at his feet as he kicked them around, his mind still on his dream.

"General, you need me?" came a raspy muttering while his brows stooped and eyes squinted.

"No, just thinking."

"Would you care for some coffee, General?"

"Do not trouble yourself, Major."

"It is my pleasure General."

Pettigrew looked to the sky wondering what General Lee had planned. He hoped he could change his mind, was aspirant that he already had. The morning brought some movement but mostly brought bewilderment and qualms about the day ahead.

His men had been at work all night, but Pettigrew still didn't know what the plan was. Where the enemy was situated on the field the way around the right was still open and Pettigrew didn't know what was wrong. He told Heth that last night, but he was inconsistent with his thoughts, was adamant about not leaving the battlefield. So Pettigrew stood in the morning, addled and in solitude.

That was how he liked it for the past few months. He didn't want to be bothered by too many people and many did not like to discuss strategy as he did. Too few believed the way he did when it came to fighting this war. Considered him too defensive minded to win the war.

Pettigrew pulled out a cigar and bit off the end, spitting it out. Lighting it with a match and with a large winnow caused

Chapter Nineteen

a fog of smoke to cast. He instructed the groom to have his horse saddled and rose to watch the sun for a moment. It crept upward as a thief tiptoes in the night. An ominous feeling came over Pettigrew that he could not explain.

His stomach distorted and gyrated about causing an unnerving feeling in his mind. He felt as though he was about to die or somebody... He shook it off and turned to his tent pushing the flap open once again.

****

All the generals for the attack were formed and laughing amongst themselves. General Longstreet stood staring across the long field at the clump of trees. He turned on his heels, walking over to the jovial bunch, all eyes turned to him. He had a hard time gathering words to say.

"Gentlemen we are going across that field right there. Artillery will precede our march up to their ridge. We tested their flanks the past couple days and found them to be sound. Pettigrew, you will be the lead element on the left of the line with Trimble following. Pickett, your divisions will be on the right of the line." Pickett showed an eager grin. "Now George, I want you to have your men turn left then straighten out a few times. That will put you on target. The objective, gentlemen, is that group of trees up yonder. We expect to split this line in two and hold that ridge. Questions?"

"Sir, just one," asked Pettigrew, "When do we step off?"

"When the artillery slows we will step off. Hopefully if they do the job right, the ridge will be yours to take."

No man had any questions, no one spoke or laughed. They stood there looking at each other, exchanging no words but some pats on the back. Longstreet stood nervously by himself staring at the ridge the Union held. General Pickett walked up next to him and stood looking at the small grouping of trees across the hazed filled field.

Pettigrew walked up to General Longstreet, "Sir if we should lose, I wish not to live." Longstreet looked deep into Pettigrew's eyes saying nothing just locking into a gaze.

"General Pettigrew, if we should win it will be on the deaths of many boys that are better than either of us."

"Amen," said Pickett.

"Amen," said Pettigrew.

"I only hope that we can sustain this battle that is coming before us," replied Longstreet looking over the vast lightly greened field before his eyes. "I only hope that the rest of our country will be able to sustain what might happen here."

Chapter Twenty

◆

Isaiah 62:6

*I have posted watchmen on your walls, O Jerusalem;
they will never be silent day or night*

July 3, 1863

The watch face read five after three in the afternoon as the drums began to beat and fifes commenced their playing. Joshua's feet instinctively moved at the sound of the rhythm, as did the rest of the Army of Northern Virginia.

"The Lord is my shepherd; I shall not want. He maketh me to lie down in green pastures; he leadeth me beside the still waters. He restoreth my soul; he leadeth me in the paths of righteousness for his name's sake. Yea, though I walk through the valley of the shadow of death, I will fear no evil; for thou art with me; thy rod and they staff they comfort me. Thou preparest a table before me in the presence of mine enemies; thou anointest me head with oil; my cup runneth over. Surely goodness and mercy shall follow me all the days of my life; and I will dwell in the house of the Lord for ever; Amen," Joshua prayed in a whispered voice.

The bayonet of his rifle shimmered and scintillated in the ardent sun. It set on his shoulder, the butt in his right hand, his left arm swinging with the movement of his body. A canteen oscillated with corresponding movements like a pendulum on a grandfather clock, water bespattering within the wooden container. On his leather belt was a pistol, fully loaded, a cartridge pouch and an officer's sword sheathed in its scabbard.

Joshua's stomach churned and rotated in perturbation. He breathed, heavy but consistent, attempting not to hyperventilate. Looking down the line all he could see was the color of the Confederacy, flags of Virginia, Alabama, Mississippi, Kentucky and many other southern states. The Confederate battle flag tiered in front of the lines as all of Joshua's vision was filled with the close to 13,000 men, all massing toward the ridge a mile away.

Their steps were heavy but concentrated. Bare feet and boots focused on the ground. They made their way up a small bluff, equipment weighing them down in the humid atmosphere. The blades of shin high grass bent over as their feet planted upon them, bowing down to the massive moving force. The eminence was small but large enough to hide them as they marched along to the beat of drums.

As the force arrived at the top, the destination of the center could be seen. The clump of trees and stone wall engulfed their minds as the point of destruction or autonomy. Just as they could see the Union position, the enemy artillery honed in on their movements and opened their cannons up and brought the world to a ghastly, thunderous exposé of death.

Some shells burst above them forming a cloud of gunpowder, raining shrapnel down on their heads. Sultry fragments burned some of the clothes and flesh of men while others continued to march. Other shells bashed into the ground fulminating large pieces of sod high into the air.

Chapter Twenty

The same explosions would send men flying, limbs going in opposite directions. They would land, dead eyes gazing up at the single wrack floating above their heads, mouths left gaping or gasping.

Joshua could see a fence line and road a quarter mile away. The wooden obstacle stood firm, a piece of resistance naturally being used to the advantage of the enemy. It would slow his men down, who already walked wearily from the shells and heat.

"Lieutenant, we gonna be slaughtered out here!" someone screamed.

"Keep moving. Take that wall and we take our freedom!" he yelled back.

"Oh my God! My leg!" another shrilled. Looking over his shoulder, he saw a young private had lost the fight with a bouncing twelve pound Napoleon, shearing off his left leg at the knee. Joshua's eyes grew wide as the teenager screamed, his body trembling and writhing in the utmost pain. The private's neck had veins popping out and eyes bulging while he breathed out his shrieks.

All the while, the men made the perpetual march toward the ridge. Scenes of this sort imbued the eyes of every soldier, not one able to turn a blind eye to it as well as being capable to stop to help. Not one man would be saved from sights of friends and brothers reaching their hands to the heavens yelling for help, knowing no relief would come to them.

This company of ragtag soldiers reached the fence line. Joshua ran up to it, "Over the top boys!" He began to climb over the wooden rails, splinters slicing into his hand. A shell burst to his side causing the fence to teeter and fall. Joshua fell face first into the sod, slowly rising. "Stay in formation! Form up on me men!"

The men formed along the side of the road, cannonade bursting through the ranks, fathers and sons plunging to the blood ridden ground.

Gray and butternut uniforms, checkered flannel shirts, blue and brown pants all crossed the road. Minie balls began to squeal past their heads and arms. Small arms began to fire on their position, some finding a target. Clothes would rip and tatter, flesh torn apart, bones breaking. Spurts of blood would mist into the air, flowing out of bodies onto the dirt and grass. Small puddles and rivers formed and streamed throughout the landscape.

The feet of soldiers still continued to move forward, even in the face of adversity and demise. The flag bearer ran ahead of the company and regiment, waving into the air only to be shot down. As the rest of the regiment reached him, another picked the battle flag off the ground, only to fall a short time after retrieving it. It incessantly occurred, the changing of hands, the endless exchange of bodies.

The regiment reached musket range and began to go through the orders of arms. They raised the muskets into the air, aimed at the enemy at the wall and pulled the heavy triggers. Clouds of powder emanated from the barrels, a hail of bullets moved towards their targets. They quickly reloaded their weapons while the enemy returned fire at their own will.

A round struck a sergeant in the stomach and as he fell his clothes and flesh had smoke rising from them. He attempted to put out the non-existent flames while he screamed and held on to the wound. The men saw this over and over but ignored it and continued to fire their weapons. One by one, the regiment began to fall, thousands of men being left on the field.

He looked to his right and saw a man running toward the wall, his hat halfway down his sword. "Follow me boys!" yelled Joshua. "Attack the wall!" he unsheathed his sword,

Chapter Twenty

dropping his musket. One hand contained his pistol, the other his saber. Pointing out both in front of him, he yelled "Charge!"

Rebel yells and screams filled the four o'clock air as the small band of soldiers made their way to the wall. Swift steps and heavy arms pointed their bodies and bayonets towards the enemy. The heat no longer plagued their minds, the humidity not a factor any more. Now it was the sea of blue uniforms that lay in front of them. As their legs were fast, the world moved slowly, seeming to stop its rotation. Although the noise was tremendous, in fact quite deafening, the ears of the army heard nothing but the sound of their hearts beating and the breathing of their lungs.

Other Confederates had already reached the clump of trees and stone wall, tossing themselves into the thick of the gray. Joshua's company was only twenty men now before reaching the wall. The sight of a general waving his sword stabbed hat in the air caused troops to rally and men to be empowered.

Joshua threw himself over the wall and stabbed a blue-belly then withdrew it. Running toward the trees, he raised his pistol cocking the hammer back, firing at a man running toward him. The enemy fell. Another came at his left and he slashed him down with his saber. A corporal stood next to him and batted away blows with his musket and jabbed with his bayonet.

A Union soldier ran at Joshua on the right. He cocked the pistol and shot the man down. Still another came and another fell, slashing and stabbing with his left, while his head moved constantly from left to right, to front and rear. His body bounced all over his position. Two others rushed at him, the blue coat on the left falling from a burst from the pistol, then the soldier on the right as Joshua swayed his arm and aimed on to the enemy.

He blocked a swinging rifle on his left and swooping the sword downward he cut the man's legs. An enemy officer raised his pistol at Joshua, but fell from the barrel of Joshua's well aimed finger. He saw a man with a bayonet pointed at him while running toward his position. He took aim with his pistol and pulled the trigger, but nothing happened. A solitary click. He cocked the hammer back again and pulled. Click.

The Yankee continued to rush at him, but stopped short and raised his rifle. Joshua realized the enemy still had a loaded musket and his sword was useless in this individual duel. As he tensed and closed his eyes, he heard the musket fire but felt nothing in the sense of pain course through his body. His eyes opened and the Yank was gone. Nate was on his left lowered his weapon. As he did, someone stabbed his protector in the back with a bayonet.

"No!"

Joshua holstered his pistol and exchanged his sword to his right hand. He ran at the enemy and thrust his body weight into the jab. The sword ran through, killing the young enemy soldier. Pulling the weapon from his body, it dripped with blood. He looked ahead of him and saw a large hand to hand fight taking place.

He rushed toward the rubble, slashing and stabbing along the way. His feet moved with quickness and arms with precision. The sword handle would glimmer in the sun, but the edge was murky with blood. Side-stepping blows and thrusting his hips into his stabs, he moved along the way to the throng of combat. Joshua looked to his right and saw a large body of blue soldiers forming. Not knowing where his company was, he attempted to yell above the battle, "Retreat!"

As the words poured out of his mouth, a shot rang out among the thousands of shots. Not louder than any other, just a blend of popping noises and loud explosions. It only

Chapter Twenty

added to the din. The shot developed a gas explosion and revealed a minie ball streaming through the air. It ripped into Joshua's left rib, spinning him around. The bones broke and flesh tore while blood spurted in the air.

He fell onto a cannon wheel, slowly sliding down to the ground. The shock of the wound enveloped his mind as his eyes grew wide and breathing grew deeper. Well aware of his surroundings, he looked to his left and watched his comrades running, walking, crawling and limping backwards toward the friendly line. One man literally ran backwards, his front still facing the enemy.

Pain grew in his heart from the scene of defeat, but soon was over taken by the pain in his side. The world seemed to crash back into real time as sights moved as commonly known and sounds filled his eardrums once again. He turned his head back to his left and noticed the enemy still lined up against the wall, pulling dead and wounded to the rear.

Joshua crawled off, trying to get to Nate. None of the soldiers around him seemed to notice or care he was crawling on his belly, the blood smearing into the sod below him. Reaching Nate, he turned him over.

"Nate?" There came no response. "Nate?" he said a little louder. Still no response came. Putting Nate's face into his neck he tried feeling for a breath. There wasn't one. "Oh God Nate… you were… always there for me when I needed you, like no one I've ever known. Thank you. I love you."

A Union lieutenant bent over and asked him some questions, but he said nothing. He didn't know if it was out of disgust or because he was unable to speak. They lay him on a stretcher and lifted him into the air, carrying him somewhere away from the field.

Joshua had no idea where he was going, until he was placed into a wagon with other soldiers. The wagon began to move and all he could see was the sky above him and passing trees. His eyes fluttered and closed then opened again. Finally all went black and all he saw were the scenes of nothingness.

His eyes rose in trepidation while his mind began to get transfixed on the whereabouts of the body, knowing he was no longer moving in a wagon. He inhaled slightly before pain coursed through him and the smell brought instant nausea to his stomach. The odor was a mixture of bile and cheese that had been rotting for days on end. Rolling over onto his right side, Joshua vomited on the ground next to him.

"We get that reaction plenty from newcomers," a woman said. Joshua looked at her as she went back to scrubbing a wound with a cake of brown soap. He said nothing in return, just lay on his back looking up at the tree above him. The leaves seemed to dance a slow mournful waltz as the slight breeze picked up in the early evening. The pain in his ribs caused him to continuously curl his toes and clench his hands while gritting the teeth in his mouth. The shallow breathing showed the intense suffering of the wound inflicted.

A Union soldier lay next to Joshua, unconscious from the wound that befell him. It was better for the Yankee to be asleep after getting his right leg removed from the top of the knee down. The pain during amputation caused the young man to pass out and he had not yet awakened from his comatose state.

The pain in Joshua's side throbbed and pulsated extreme labors throughout the body. The light flickered a little as his eyelids flashed open and shut. Finally the world became dark to him as the sound of his breathing put him under a deep trance within the caliginous world. Amidst the darkness, images of his farm came to his eyes as well as his sister and mother.

They were weeping, handkerchiefs mopping the tears and eyes gazed upon a body. The body wore a blue uniform. As Joshua came behind them, he touched their shoulders. His mother's hand grasped his while upon her shoulder and

Chapter Twenty

she turned her head up at him. "He's doin' just fine," she said. Joshua said nothing back, just looked at the Blue soldier in bewilderment as to his identity.

Another man with blond hair wearing a cavalry cap walked up to the dead soldier and removed his hat, brushing his hair behind his ears. This man wore no uniform, but had on a business suit. "He's fine," Anderson's mother said again. The business man looked at the two women and nodded his head, then left the scene.

Joshua's eyes flashed open, then closed again, the scene now a weeping willow tree, fully in bloom.

The green leaves and branches hung low to the ground and he sat upon the bow sipping a lemonade drink. His sister lay upon her back reading a book to him as he sat slowly falling asleep. A voice called out to him in the dream, "How are you Sergeant?"

"I am no sergeant, I am a lieutenant," Joshua replied. The smell of rotting and decaying flesh entered his nostrils, bowels open and feces drying swelled the inner being of his nose. His eyelids darted to the upper regions of his eye socket as a man was talking to the Yankee to his right. The blurry vision took a moment to come into focus. When they did, his mouth gaped, for it was the man from his dream.

The man wore a hat, blocking the sun, the blue uniform worn and dirty. The blond hair extended down before being wrapped behind the ears. His sword draped off to his side, the metal clanging as he shifted weight. "I asked how you were, Sergeant?"

"Oh..just fine. They say I'll make it, but as you see..lost my leg."

"Well, better a leg than a life, I guess," the man responded.

"Your friend is fine Captain," spat out Anderson.

The blonde man looked at him and scowled before sarcastically responding, "That is what he said, thank you, Johnny Reb."

"No...I mean.... your other friend...that died."
"What are you talking about?" the man demanded.
"What is your name Captain?"
"Captain Spalding," the man retorted.

Chapter Twenty-One

◆

Zechariah 1:8

During the night I had a vision, and there before me was a man riding a red horse...Behind him were red, brown and white horses.

July 3, 1863

"Yes sir, General Merritt instructed me to join you," said James.
"Very well...welcome to Michigan." replied General Custer.
"Sir?"
"This brigade is from Michigan, son. Where you abide at?"
"New York."
"I won't hold that against you, I guess. You and your men stick by with the 7th Michigan over on the right. "
"Yes, General."
James turned the horse by pulling with his right hand, directing the bit in the mouth. General Custer rode with him to introduce him to the Michigan regiment.

"That is Stuart out there, am sure of it. At eleven he fired four shots. Of course this alerted General Gregg and I knew there was going to be a fight. I wanted this one, so naturally I requested permission to join his fight," explained Custer.

"Naturally," replied James.

"So General Gregg put John McIntosh and me on this farm to block 'em."

"The Rummel Farm, sir."

"Beg your pardon?"

"I am a map maker..that includes asking locals the name of certain areas. This farm I guess belongs to John Rummel."

"Well, whomever, we are going to fight here." It only took a few minutes to reach the 7th and General Custer trotted his horse to the commanding officer. "Captain, this is Colonel D'Antonmann of the 7th Michigan Cavalry. Colonel this is Captain....," Custer looked questioningly.

"Spalding."

"Right! Captain Spalding. He will be joining you in this fight. He and the men General Merritt send to reinforce us. Enjoy their companionship for the time being."

"Yes, General Custer," replied D'Antonmann.

Custer left the two men sitting atop their mounts, the pleasantries of introduction being surmised through small conversation. The men were watching off in the distance the Rebel cavalry advance on the skirmish line of the 5th Michigan Cavalry.

James pulled out his glasses and looked on the line, now not that far away. He could see Stuart's men attempting to pin down the Union. He knew that the enemy wanted to swing over Cress Ridge. The left flank was vital to this fight and Stuart would know that.

"They are certainly putting up a devil of a fight."

"The 5th are tough and are armed with the Spencer repeat," replied D'Antonmann.

Chapter Twenty-One

Continuing to glass the field, James watched the enemy withdraw. He had a feeling they would try again, only this time in greater numbers. An earth shattering noise came from behind him and he turned in the saddle. Looking behind him, he scrunched his brow. "That is the main line. Them Rebs are attacking the main body as well."

"I guess we can't let 'em pass here then can we," replied D'Antonmann.

James looked at his watch, the gold gleaming in the midday sun. "One o'clock." The sound from behind them was exasperating while the image in front of them was raising the acid in his stomach. The 5th Michigan was falling back from their skirmish line and the enemy was attacking directly into the Union Cavalry.

Custer's horse galloped ferociously, the hooves raised a thunderous applause of noise and caused the earth to shower down sod. The steed skidded to a halt and the General swiftly unsheathed his sword raising the blade high into the air.

"Come on you Wolverines!" he shouted.

"What's a wolverine?" asked a sergeant to Spalding.

"Don't know, but let's move!"

A hard kick to the ribs forced the horse to a stumbling start, another lick put the trusted animal at a full gallop. Over seven hundred horses and men began to charge at each other at a full run. The sound of horse hooves overwhelmed the noise of cannons behind the battle. All the tumult of stampeding horses, cannon shot bursting, muskets and rifles, battle cries and screams of wounded and metal on metal striking each other mixed together in a barrage of ear piercing, law defying din.

The horses collided point blank at a fence line on the farm. Carbines fired across the fence, bullets streaming past some and becoming embedded in the bodies of others. James pulled his pistol out and pulled the hammer back. He took aim at an enemy trooper, squeezed the trigger.

A powder smoke came forth from the barrel, a projectile spewing from out of the smoke, killing the horseman. From target to target, kill to wounding, James repeated this action.

Custer's men had amassed at the fenceline and broke some of it down. James and his company crossed the line with the 7th Michigan. Holstering his pistol, he retrieved his sword and slashed a man across the arm. The enemy clutched his wound, turning his horse and riding away. A second enemy trooper charged at Jim, swinging his sword toward James. The young Captain avoided the steel blade by lowering his head, while simultaneously cutting through the air with his own sword, catching the enemy in the throat, the artery spewing out blood.

The Virginians began to turn their horses, while gripping their pistols and swords and adrenaline. The regiment divided into three small columns as they attempted to go to the enemy's flank.

The mass of men and waves of horses collided on the grassy field. The heat of the day increased a hundred fold with the heat of the battle. Either sabers clashed or rifles fired, but the result was the same, blood on the ground. Horses toppled end over end, crushing the rider below, while crying out in their own pain. Saddles grew loose, tossing men to the stomping hooves below. The screams not being heard by men, just being lost in the intense tumultuous battle.

James slashed and stabbed, cut and pierced but a sword grazed his left arm. Crying out in pain, he came across his body with his saber shoving the blade into the body of his nemesis. More enemy riders came into the intense battle, outnumbering the Union.

"Fall back!" came a cry from Custer. It shouted from man to man. "Retreat!"

Yanking the bit in the horse's mouth, James turned it around. "On me men! Follow me out of this mess!" The men from the various regiments that made up James' group fol-

Chapter Twenty-One

lowed their captain out of the fray. He struck at extended swords and blocked blows while galloping from within the fight. The retreat from the Michiganders was wild and disorderly, all trying to fall back to their lines with their lives.

One by one they reached the safety of the fence row, the noise of battle being replaced by the babble of galloping enemy horsemen behind them. The sabers were lifted high above their heads and their Rebel yell higher than their swords. Cannons began to rumble and explosions attempted to impede the advance of the enemy. Shells and canister shot rained down on the field, but to no avail. The enemy was riding much too quickly to have artillery do any damage.

"Come on you Wolverines!" shouted Custer once again. James saw remnants of the 7th Michigan joined by the 1st Michigan led by Colonel Town. They rushed toward the Rebel cavalry. His head sunk and shook, then he pointed his saber toward the ensuing battle.

"Charge!"

The two columns of men approached each other at a gallop, increasing in speed the closer they came. As quick as a rifle came fire. The two armies met in the middle of the field, crashing together in a loud percussion of sound, neither side backing away. Horses turned over, men fell, blood poured and screams gasped in wheezy breaths.

James thrust his right hand forward, stabbing a body with the tip of his blade. An enemy rider came from behind, pinching his left leg between the horses. He blocked a downward thrust of the arm and James grabbed the back of the collar, strong-arming the Rebel to the crowded ground below.

Captain Spalding and his gallant men with General Custer and his Wolverines fought ferociously on the center of battle. In the midst of the fight, McIntosh's brigade could be heard on the right flank of the enemy as well as the left. The enemy's left flank began to cave as the Union came from the Lott house.

"Captain! My leg! I been hit!" screamed a sergeant. The sergeant was on James' right and was slowly falling off the horse to be trampled below. The reins fell out of his hand and the upper torso began to slip out of the saddle. As one foot came out of the stirrup, Spalding's hand gripped the man's jacket. With all of his strength, he pulled the young sergeant onto his horse, the body laying across his saddle. Producing his sword again, he slashed his way out of the battle, calling his men as he did.

The Confederates began to fall back after being attacked on all three sides of the battlefield. James reached a small bluff atop the farm. He turned and saw his men following him, no one killed but some saber wounds and minie ball scratches. In the distance he saw General Custer walking, after losing his second horse. James pulled his watch from his tunic pocket. "One forty-five. Simply amazing."

He lowered himself down from the mount before pulling down the sergeant. James applied a tourniquet to Nichol's leg and bandaged the seeping wound.

"Oh God this hurts!" screamed the young man, gasping for air.

"Sergeant. I will get you to the main road."

"Sir. I don't much care where, no disrespect tended. I just hurt!"

"Sergeant, the nearest road is the Low Dutch Road. That will not suffice, but the Hanover Road will be crowded with ambulances. I will get you to a hospital."

"Yes, sir."

The captain and a platoon lieutenant lifted the man onto James' horse once again, as he cried out in agony. Mounting the horse himself and kicking the weary animal, they moved toward the road. With each bump came a scream and each thump came a cry. Finally the sergeant became silent from the pain.

"Doctor! I need a doctor!" yelled out James.

Chapter Twenty-One

No response came from the crowd of men and streams of wagons. An open cart came by and teamed past the captain. He kicked the animal again and it lurched forward.

"Is this an ambulance cart?" asked James.

"Sure is."

"Where are you heading?"

"I ain't. I'm waitin'"

"For what?" questioned Spalding.

"You hear all them booms out there?"

"Yes!" Spalding answered impatiently.

"Well..there are gonna be a lot of wounded."

"Are you in the Army man?"

"No sir. Just a townsman from Gettysburg."

"Can you take my friend to a hospital?"

"Um...I suppose so. Put 'em in the back."

"I thank you kindly," James replied in frustration as two men took the sergeant from atop his horse and placed him in the empty cart.

"Now I'm heading toward the Union main body. There are plenty of hospitals on the Baltimore Pike. I'll take 'em there."

"I am in debt to you sir," he said, finally settling down.

"Just want this war to end," the man replied looking into the distance.

"We all do," Jim said quietly and with that the driver slapped the horses with the reins giving the signal to move out. "Company! We are going to head southwest. There is a creek and a little shade there. The center seems to be getting all the action right now. At least that is where the cannons are firing. We will rest the horses for a couple hours before moving on to General Merritt and meet up with a reserve brigade. Hopefully by then, the battle up there will be over. Our ammunition is short and so is our readiness."

"Captain, what about Sergeant Nichols?"

"What about him?"

"Well...sir...are we going to go see him?"

"Lieutenant Marks and I will stop and find him. Other than that, Lieutenant Chapel will lead you men back to General Merritt. Any other questions?" There was no response. "Very well, move out."

The animals were slow to respond from the command of the riders. Grudgingly and reluctantly they did as they were told, moving their powerful legs once again. Some of the horses heads pulled at the reins, wanting more slack and wanting the journey to end. Others bobbed their heads up and down, jerking against the bit in their mouths. They whinnied, they grunted, and a few tried to bite the legs of their riders.

The green countryside was plush and plentiful, with the attempt to divert eyes from the occasional hospital or wounded straggler it was actually a pleasant ride. Closing his eyes for a short moment, James imagining the war being over and he riding next to his wife. He could almost hear her laughing if it weren't for the enormously loud cannon barrage occurring in the distance. His eyes opened when Lieutenant Chapel began to speak.

"We sort of left General Custer hanging back there. He did not even know we left."

"Yes, he did."

"How could he?"

"I waved at him before we left. He waved back, then saluted."

"Oh."

"I would not have abandoned my post without orders, Lieutenant."

"Of course not, sir. Sir, what happens if with all that clamoring up there, it just so happens that the South breaks the line?"

Chapter Twenty-One

"Well....that is why we must get back to Merritt. But the horses will not make it there unless we rest them and get them some water."

"Of course, sir."

James gave the order to dismount and to cool the horses before watering them. He walked over to a tall oak tree providing a shade to sit down under. His back propped against the coarse bark and he slid down to his backside, while unfolding a map he took his jacket off.

"Private McFarland, please bring me a handkerchief from my satchel." James rolled up his sweat stained, dirt riddled white shirt sleeve while staring at the map. His eyes went from the map to his left arm, blood slowly trickling down the muscular limb. The private handed him the cloth and James wrapped it around the slight wound. Rolling his sleeve down and replacing his tunic, his sight became focused on the map again.

After a short while, the horses began to drink out of the babbling creek. The moving water and the heat combined to induce a sweet lullaby that put heavy eyelids to bed and darkness to his retinas. The world stopped if only for a brief moment to give that sweet relief from reality that every soldier needs.

While in his brief slumber, the cannonade ceased in the distance northeast of their position. A corporal and private argued amongst themselves, the bickering becoming quite loud. The contention of words came to such a volume that it woke James from his brief sleep. "What is the problem, Corporal?"

"Sorry sir. I thought you should know that the cannon fire stopped."

"What! How long ago?"

"Half an hour, sir."

"Why did no one wake me?"

"That is what the argument was about, sir."

"Hmm?"

"I thought we ought to wake you, the private here wanted you to sleep."

"I should have been alerted, you are correct Corporal. Saddle your horses and form up. Private come here," replied James as the corporal saluted them and moved out.

"Yes, sir? I'm sorry about that. I thought...."

"You are in no trouble son. Thank you for caring about me enough to let me sleep. You are a fine trooper, a fine man. Never let anyone tell you otherwise."

"Yes, sir. Thank you." The smiling private ran away to attend to his horse as Lieutenant Chapel came running up.

"Captain, the men are almost ready and formed."

"Thank you Lieutenant."

"Orders, sir?"

"Directly west of our position is the Baltimore Pike. We will take that north and hopefully run into General Merritt. There is a lot of musket fire going on over there. We need to get riding."

"What if them Rebs break through?"

"Hopefully we can intercept and lend a hand then. The cannons have pretty much been silent for forty-five minutes. Let's move out, Lieutenant."

"Yes, sir."

The cavalry mounted their somewhat rested horses and moved across the creek. The water splashed upward and sloshed outward, spewing on the riding boots and horses' legs that both soaked up the cooler substance. On the other side, the riders nudged the animals to a trot attempting to get a bit faster to the Baltimore Pike, a quarter mile away.

As they began to reach the road, the houses that were established nearby now became make shift hospitals. The road was jammed with carts and men going toward Gettysburg and other men hobbling around. They turned

Chapter Twenty-One

northward toward Spangler's spring and picked up the pace to a slow gallop.

The company of men and horses blended into the mix of supply wagons and soldiers looking like they were swimming upstream like a school of salmon. Cries of victory began to be yelled from infantry soldiers. James pulled his mount off the side of the road and saw a soldier yelling.

"You there, soldier! What is happening?" shouted James.

"Haven't you heard Captain? We beat them Rebs back. They attacked in force on the center but we handled them real good. They fallin' back right now!"

"Thank you, son. Lieutenant Chapel!" he shouted as the lieutenant came riding up to him.

"Yes, sir?"

"Take the men on to General Merritt. Send him my compliments. I am going to check out a few of the hospitals nearby to look for the sergeant."

"Yes, Captain."

"Move out, men."

James commanded his horse to move and began to look around. The amount of supplies, wagons, men, cannons and horses overwhelmed his eyes. He began to wonder how he was going to find his sergeant. Then as if a cool breeze turned his head, he saw a familiar wagon and the man driving it. It was the man he had spoken with earlier.

Dismounting his horse and performing a quick release knot on a low hanging branch, he walked over to the farmhouse. The house was white, obviously worn from weather with the paint fading and chipping away. The shutters were closed except for one on the first floor near the front entrance. The stone walkway had been trampled over and some pieces of stone either removed or misplaced.

Men sat upon the railing leaning up against the post, bandages over their heads and eyes. The front porch had soldiers lying shoulder to shoulder with only a small path in front of the door and between their feet and house. The yard was littered with bodies, limbs, stretchers and equipment. A woman went from man to man, cleaning their wounds.

James, himself, went from man to man scanning their faces as he looked for the young sergeant. Each face, a new look of terror or pain, each man crying out or returning a lifeless gaze. His stomach began to feel uneasy, his nerves and emotions overcoming him.

Out of the medical chaos and calamity came a familiar face, the face of Sergeant Nichols. Next to him was a rebel soldier seemingly unconscious. James walked over to the men and noticed the missing leg. Apparently not unconscious, the rebel man began speaking to James, yet his eyes remained shut.

"Your friend is fine."

James retorted a sarcastic reply, but instantly regretted it.

"What's your name, Captain?" asked the enemy.

"Captain Spalding. What is yours?"

"Lieutenant Anderson."

Chapter Twenty-Two

James 1:4

Perseverance must finish its work so that you may be mature and complete, not lacking anything.

July 3, 1863

The hooves pounced on the ground as a mountain lion on prey. The heartbeat of the movement like a clock never missing a tick. Sod soared about like rain on a windy day. The mane blew from the rushing wind caused by swift legs and powerful muscles. Its breathing, was ever so calibrated to keep in perfect rhythm of the fast gallop.

The artillery from the southern line was silent and General Hancock rushed forward to check the lines. His elegant uniform bounced along with him in the saddle, the brass buttons fastened all the way to the collar bone. His mustache and chin neatly groomed, not a hair out of place.

His hands pulled back upon the reins and the bit applied pressure on the horse's mouth, commanding it to stop. Hancock looked upon the Union line, watching the conglomeration of men stack up against the stone wall. Off in the distance the enemy stretched for what seemed like miles wide, all heading directly for the center. The union artillery began to spout off at the mouth, attempting to stop the impeding force.

"Steady boys! Only fire when you see their eyes!" yelled Hancock. He rode up and down the center near a patch of trees. To his left he saw the Eighteenth Massachusetts performing the manual of arms. He could hear the drums of the enemy beating ferociously in the heat as he sat atop his horse in amazement at the courage of the enemy.

"Sir, the cannons are firing as ordered," said an orderly.

"Good. Make sure they concentrate on the center of their force. If we can cut them down from the center out, we have a good chance at dwindling their numbers."

"Yes, sir."

The Confederate line continued to advance on the Union position through the torrential downpour of cannons and rainclouds of gunpowder. Hancock watched them knock down a fence along the road in front of him. The cannons focused and zeroed in on the fence row, sending men and parts flying and sod and wood splinters soaring.

As the enemy inched closer, their numbers declined, but they remained steadfast in the cause. Regimental leaders gave the order to open fire with their muskets. They unleashed a deadly array of fire, the carnage unfolding in front of Hancock's eyes. The Rebels stopped and raised their rifles and returned fire. Bullets flew through the air, streaming through and past men. General Hancock felt an intense heat and sharp pain in his left side and began to slide off his horse.

An orderly ran to the General's aid and caught him before he fell to the ground. "My God, General. Is it bad?"

"Get me a doctor...wait...do not bring him here."

"Sir?"

"It is much too dangerous right now."

"General, we must get you out!"

Chapter Twenty-Two

"No. Just stop the bleeding for God's sake. We must beat back the enemy!"

****

He kicked and scratched the ground with his boot, the dirt moving and swirling about like a bowl of batter with a spoon. His stomach was uneasy, his head heavy with thought while dangling arms clasped behind his back. The artillery had stopped, the musket fire now intermittent. No true word of the battle.

A wildly riding horseman, screaming like a banshee, approached the major. "We beat 'em back! We got 'em rebs on the run!" He handed the major a piece of paper. The major, in turn, came to him smirking, a glistening in his eyes.

"General Meade."

"Major?"

"Sir, the rebels are retreating back to their lines. We have stood firm on the center."

"Good, very good."

"Sir. General Hancock has been severely wounded."

"Good God! Will he survive?"

"I...it does not say, sir," the major replied looking down at the paper that had been handed to him.

"Let us pray he does. We cannot afford to lose Winfield."

"Sir they want orders. Should they push on and pursue the enemy?"

"No! They will have set up positions of defense on their ridge. It would prove costly. No Major, tell them to hold."

"Yes, sir."

Relief swelled up into the General's mind almost causing the illusion of a coolness to set in the temperature. His breathing was less shallow, the air seemed fresh to him.

"Major."

"Yes, General."

"When you are finished, get a wire to the President."

"Saying what General?"

"State our victory upon today's action. Anticipating more action from enemy, will update at later time."

"Yes, General."

"I need a courier!" yelled Meade.

A scrawny young private came running. His nose pointed out and high cheek bones gave the picture of an elf, his ears back on his head. "Yes, sir?"

Meade looked at the boy, scanning him up and down. "Son, go tell General Geary's aides to support their lines on the flanks. I expect a final effort from the enemy on the flanks. Have General Geary spread the order to General Sykes on the left flank. They might think we are weakened there after the attack on the center. Move!"

"Sir, it's like Fredricksburg, only we got the wall!" someone shouted.

Meade paid no attention to the shouts of victory, the cries of joy or the screams of defeating the enemy. He instead went behind a wagon, finding a chair and a quiet location for a few lonely seconds. He removed his cap and looked to the sky, breathing out a long hot breath. "Thank You," he muttered.

Once again the duties called out to him and Meade lifted himself from the chair. He stopped briefly before rounding the corner of the wagon. General Meade wiped some tears and straightened his smile. "Who is moving those replacements in?"

****

General Pettigrew looked through his field glasses, rage building up inside of him. The pain of watching his soldiers march to their deaths and the humility of defeat began to work on his emotions. The pain of watching the enemy

Chapter Twenty-Two

retain the field and the wound in his hand caused him to retreat back within his mind. Cannon fodder was within his pupils, a shell bursting to his left raining dirt and grass over his body. His face tightened, the muscles of his chin and cheeks retracting. The teeth within his jaw clenched together with such intensity it seemed a tooth would break.

"Would someone tell me what happened? Where is the artillery?" Pettigrew yelled and cursed God. Rounds still whizzed past his head. "I want fire support for those boys coming back!"

No one replied, just watched in awe of this mad man stomping about, kicking dirt into the air. His screams fell upon God to decipher at times. "Somebody find Pickett, those are his boys up there, we need information."

A major took off on his horse to find General Pickett, leaving the brooding man without a word. After several minutes of loud obscenities, General Pettigrew stood in silence watching the enemy ridge. His eyes burrowed deep within their sockets, the brows on his head scrunched to the point of being in unison.

"General Pettigrew," came a raspy, whispered voice.

Pettigrew turned slowly. "General, sir what happened?"

"Our boys....they hit the wall..." Pickett began, attempting not to sob, the words coming out intermittently between breaths. "...not enough left to take them trees."

"My God, George, we have no one left do we?"

A long pause came, the breath of the world being held, the balance of the atmosphere on a string. "No... we do not." Pickett replied, his eyes fluttering away from any contact before rivers of tears began to stream down his face. All the men around let out a gasp at one time, in the effect of one's stomach being struck with a sharp force.

"Someone please take General Pickett back to his quarters," whispered Pettigrew, staring into absolutely nothing. "I'll be in my tent should anybody need me."

Pettigrew mounted a nearby horse and began to ride back to his camp in heartache. His body trembled in anger and fear, and his mind flashed between scenes of dead men and dead children. His own eyes began to swell, but he squashed the feeling, while the retinas were filled with sights of horror, ghastly images of dissolution and decomposition.

His camp was empty of jovial moods and flickering playing cards. All eyes turned to Pettigrew as he dismounted, paused shortly before entering his tent, and glowering eyes sent the message to all he was not to be disturbed.

Inside, the humidity was stifling but he closed the flap anyway. He threw his hat on his cot, unsheathed his sword and raised his clenched fists to his head in a stabbing position, then paused. His chest rose heavily, his rage sweltering to the surface and he stared at his hat. Slowly his hands fell and the sword within their grasp. "Too much destruction today," he said softly to himself.

The major dashed his head inside the tent. "General Heth requests your presence sir. Sir, you must get your hand looked at. It is bleeding quite bad sir."

"I will see to it son, do not worry about me. Look to yourself for this day is a sad one."

****

"....and General Pickett reports his whole division has been destroyed and...."

"No more Major. I do not believe my heart can withstand any more."

"My apologies, General Heth."

"No, no. Apologies are not necessary. I am pleased to have your service and overjoyed you are in fine health today. Please leave me to my thoughts and when General Pettigrew arrives we are not to be disturbed."

Chapter Twenty-Two

The tent flap closed with a brush of canvas as the major left Heth to himself. No faces in the crack, no raps on the wooden post. He buried his forehead into the palm of this left hand and began to sob uncontrollably. For what could possibly have been eternity, but was a few minutes, General Heth wept.

"My Heavenly Father. Please take care of all those fine men," he whispered then inhaled a sniffle. "And please forgive my arrogance. I have allowed foolish pride to find its way into my heart."

Silence overcame the cries to God. Heth could hear voices outside but didn't want to listen. He just sat in a sunken position in his chair and rocked himself gently, listening to the whisper of breeze filled leaves speak and the soft wooden chair whisper. The voice he truly wanted to hear remained silent, not answering the many questions. Perhaps the answer was the silence, he thought.

A small tap on the post broke the conversation with the inanimate objects and entering the tent was Pettigrew. Heth could not rise or make eye contact.

"General?"

"Please sit down with me Jim?"

Pettigrew paused at the use of his shortened name before pulling a chair beside him. They sat in silence for several minutes before General Heth broke it.

"We will hold our position until we can gather the wounded. Then we will retreat back to the mountain behind us at General Lee's orders. We will keep moving until we reach Virginia."

"Yes, sir."

"I have killed us!"

"Sir......," replied Pettigrew, shaking his head.

"Oh, yes. I have destroyed our army. I am very glad that General Jackson is not here to see this."

"If General Jackson was here, we would be having a victory celebration. I am not the general he was sir."

"None of us are."

"General Heth....you cannot expect to win every battle. Sir, I have ridden through the camp. We are bruised, not dead. These men know the cost of freedom and I assure you they lay no blame on you."

"I made them march to their death on that first day. It was my decision to believe they were just militia. I am to blame for all this agony. Listen Jim! Hear the cries of the soldiers outside this tent. We have killed the very thing we swore to. I have killed men because of my decision to act that first day. I am to blame Jim, and I alone."

"We are soldiers, General Heth. We all march to our death. We all march to the beyond and we all march afterwards. In peace....we march. In war..we march. In faith...we march. No man knowingly beseeches the intolerable trial of endurance, but soldiers step in cadence headlong into that endurance. We have been taught to persevere and to overcome."

"Your words have not fallen on deaf ears."

"Sir, I am going to leave you with this. If I was to know the future, I never would have gone to be a lawyer, instead I would have gone to be a soldier. Not because my life as a soldier is better or worse, but because my decisions of being a lawyer have sometimes been too great of a burden. I have taken men on as clients that should not have had my representation and others I could do nothing to help, yet were innocent. But Sir, we put on this uniform everyday not because we look good in it, but it is because it fits us. If I was to know the future....I would still follow you."

Chapter Twenty-Three

John 5:24

...he has crossed over from death to life

July 3, 1863

"To what friend are you referring?"
"You just had one die didn't you?"
"We have all had friends die," replied James.
" Just the other day. He was close to you," said Joshua.
"How do you know all this?"
"God told me."
"God...sure. The same God that allowed my brother-in-law to die, right?"
"How does blaming God bring him back? I can't tell ya why these things happen, but they do."
James sat on the ground next to Joshua, one leg flat in front of him, the other raised slightly with his foot planted flat on the ground and knee lifted above it. "I had so much faith in God before this."
"Strange things happen in this life. The only possible explanation for this is God wants to perfect us. We are to

continue the act in faith," responded Joshua, coughing as he did so.

"Are you in pain?"

"Great amount...." Anderson gasped.

"Maybe I can get the doctor....well drink this actually." James pulled out Matt's flask and lifted Joshua's head to the spout. He poured some of the amber liquid into the man's mouth.

"Whiskey?" coughed Anderson.

"Yes. Drink it."

James allowed Joshua to remain silent for a moment. The whiskey coursed through his body, through the blood stream, warming the insides and dulling the pain in his side. After his breathing became normal, James began to speak again.

"I thought God was on my side," James mumbled.

"God is not choosing sides in the squabbles of his people. He did not choose this fight but rather we did. We chose to go to war from futility, ignorance, and the inability to listen to God. God is on both our sides. The body count is no one's fault but our own," replied Joshua. "No matter what we must go through in this life, we can't lose hope Cap'n. God wants to make us stronger, not weakin' us."

"Or we are like ants to him," Jim said with a sardonic voice.

"He does not crush us. We crush ourselves."

"How do I move past this when I am so angry?"

"Anger is an emotion....it's from God... but to give in, to let it change you, is from the enemy," replied Joshua, his breath becoming erratic once again.

"You did not answer *how*?"

"Each of us has to find a way to cope. You...are a strong man....for...your...men. Stop feeling sorry for yourself."

"How dare you...." James replied bitterly.

"We've all had friends die!"

Chapter Twenty-Three

"How does that help me!" James looked at him with scornful eyes.

"The answer is sometimes not....what you expect."

"Lieutenant..." James said, but Joshua had become silent, his eyelids flickering. "Lieutenant?"

"God loves you no matter what you decide," said Joshua coughing. Blood spit out from his mouth, falling on his shirt, staining it red.

James sat up to a kneeling position and grasped Joshua's hand. "I am right here Lieutenant."

"Capt'n. You're strong...."

James continued to hold Joshua's hand, clasping both hands around the one so limp. "Don't...let this keep...you from....paradise."

"Easy Lieutenant. Do not speak, save your strength for the surgeon."

"In God's hands..." whispered Anderson, "we are...all...."

"All what?"

No reply came, just heavy labored breathing from Lieutenant Anderson. Down the row of wounded soldiers laid Captain Gordon of Joshua's regiment. He had watched the captain hover over his lieutenant as tears had filled Spalding's eyes. "He's right," Gordon muttered to himself.

James was clasping Joshua's hand as the breathing turned to wheezing, then turned to gasping. The air flow in and out of the lungs was becoming shorter and less frequent. Joshua could speak no words, form no thought, and he could squeeze Spalding's hand no longer. As James watched the man's eyes glaze over, he heard the gasping turn to one long gurgling exhale.

"Lieutenant?" James whispered. "Lieutenant?" he said a little louder.

Captain James Spalding patted Joshua's hand and returned it to his side. Leaning back on his heels, he pushed off his knees and rose, nodding his head at this Confederate soldier.

Anderson walked past the white fence outside the house, walking through the gate entrance, the hinges squeaking as he did. The cobblestone walk led to the porch steps and he climbed them, his boots thumping along the wood. His hand grazed the railing while he walked along the wrap-around porch of the home, following it to the back steps.

The yard in the back was plush green, a creek babbling in the latter most part. A weeping willow tree stood on the left corner of the yard while the creek bent around it. There below was a woman dressed in a white dress, a bonnet and veil covering her head. Her white satin gloves contained a book, the pages lifting on the edges from the cool breeze.

Anderson's feet led him toward her, his boots crunching on the grass producing a scratching noise of crisp green sod. His steps were slow and methodically designed to tread lightly in her presence. While he inched closed to her, his heart beat faster, but his nerves were excited, calm. Upon reaching her, she lifted her veil revealing her glorious shining smile.

"Sit." she said. "Have some lemonade."
"Thank you."
"Would you like me to read to you?"
"That would be lovely."
"Welcome home dear brother."

Epilogue

Psalm 116:7

*Be at rest once more,
O my soul, for the Lord has been good to you*

November 19, 1863

The chill in the air was quite different than earlier days of heat and humidity. The steps leading down from the train seemed as though they could have frost. The man stepped lightly with his boots in high shine and light blue pants crisply pressed. The sword on his side would have shimmered and gleamed even without a sun. At the bottom of the steps he turned and raised his left hand to a lady stepping out after him.

Her dress was wide at the base but narrowed as it climbed her body. It rippled and danced with every step of her feet and the fabric swayed to and fro from the light breeze. A heavy plaid shawl draped over her shoulders to keep in the warmth of her body while here head was covered, not with a bonnet but, with a woolen scarf.

The man hailed a horse and closed carriage to drive them. Inside they sat across from one another and gave polite, nervous smiles while riding in silence. Many words had been exchanged on the train, but now the only conversation taking place was the bustle of busy sidewalks and extreme din of crowded streets, as all words were lost in the abyss of mourning and dissolution. The click clop of hooves on stone preceded them all the way until the carriage could pass no more.

The amount of people was uncountable to fathom in the human minds. The man once more aided the woman in exiting their mode of transportation as they now moved by walking toward their destination. Her left arm wrapped around his right while walking slowly through the crowd.

The two reached the top of a small knoll where reporters were gathered and minute bands of gatherers waited with impatient anticipation. A newspaperman ran toward the two and begged a story.

"Were you here soldier?"

"Captain."

"Oh, sorry. Were you here for the battle Captain?"

"I was."

"Were you injured?"

"Yes."

"Is this your wife?"

"No."

"What is your name?"

"Captain James Spalding."

"Whom were you with in battle?"

"General Buford's cavalry."

"Who is this with you?"

"The widow of a dear departed friend and comrade and she wishes to be left alone by weasels such as yourself."

"How did your friend die?"

"The way in which we are dedicating the cemetery today. Now please, leave us. Let us have our privacy."

Epilogue

The reporter saw a hint of battle wear in James' eyes that made him back off. James and Barbara strolled together around the grounds attempting to put into imagination the setting of the cemetery. As hard as they tried and as much as they spoke, neither could see its magnitude and beauty.

All their walking led them to a proscenium and podium set up on the outskirts of town. From there they viewed the pomp and glory of parades and dignitaries waving their hands. The entirety of these actions led to the platform, while keynote speakers began to walk up to speak.

"James."

"Yes, maam."

"May I ask you a question that I have been quite fearful to ask?"

"Of course."

"Is my husband in peace, do you think?"

"I do not think, but I know that Matt is at peaceful rest in heaven!"

"How do you know?"

"A friend told....God told me."

"Really? I....I..do not understand," she said softly, questions in her eyes.

"It is really nothing to be worried about, just know that he is fine," replied James.

"I believe you."

The two stood there while the chilling air swirled around the large crowd. A man stood on the platform speaking for an innate amount of time. The people began to grow restless the longer the man spoke. Shifting from foot to foot in order to relieve pressure and release the pain due to standing in once place for so many hours.

"Who is this speaking?" asked Barbara.

"I do not know him," replied James.

"He is Edward Everett," whispered a man standing by them.

"Oh...well.. thank you," said Barbara. "Who is that?" she asked in a whisper leaning over to Jim.

"No idea," he whispered back.

The orator Everett ended his speech and Jim pulled out his watch. Over two hours he had been speaking, two hours of standing still in the cold. Spalding's shoulders stiffened as he saw a new man take the podium, a tall dark man with a large black stovepipe top hat. Even though the crowd stood anxiously, James stood still.

There was something about the President's presence, almost ominous. It was a commanding yet delicate feeling, a reverence yet gentle sentiment. President Lincoln had a walk, a stride about him that told people he was strong but weary. An expression which portrayed a general atmosphere of care and charge. His long lanky legs gave the story of a man that could handle the trials and tribulations of a nation.

A hush and awe came over James as he watched the President shake hands. Even though he was just a man, he felt like there was something more. A kindred spirit. An altruistic ear. A set of shoulders to lay your burdens on. The President faced the crowd and scanned over them. Taking a heavy breath and letting out the warm stream releasing the fear, releasing the anguish and letting go of the pain of a nation at war, he spoke.

Four score and seven years ago........

ARMY OF NORTHERN VIRGINIA

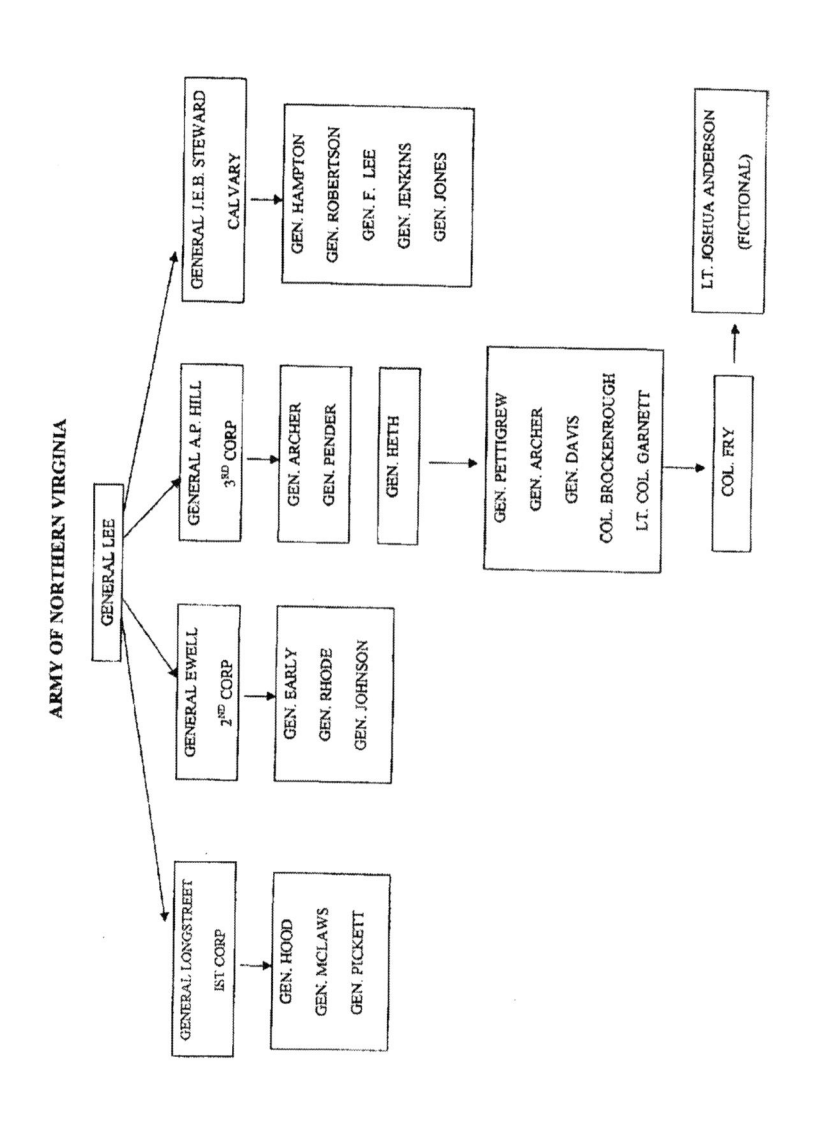

GENERAL LEE

- **GENERAL LONGSTREET** — 1ST CORP
  - GEN. HOOD
  - GEN. MCLAWS
  - GEN. PICKETT

- **GENERAL EWELL** — 2ND CORP
  - GEN. EARLY
  - GEN. RHODE
  - GEN. JOHNSON

- **GENERAL A.P. HILL** — 3RD CORP
  - GEN. ARCHER
  - GEN. PENDER
  - GEN. HETH → GEN. PETTIGREW / GEN. ARCHER / GEN. DAVIS / COL. BROCKENROUGH / LT. COL. GARNETT → COL. FRY → LT. JOSHUA ANDERSON (FICTIONAL)

- **GENERAL J.E.B. STEWARD** — CALVARY
  - GEN. HAMPTON
  - GEN. ROBERTSON
  - GEN. F. LEE
  - GEN. JENKINS
  - GEN. JONES

ARMY OF THE POTOMAC

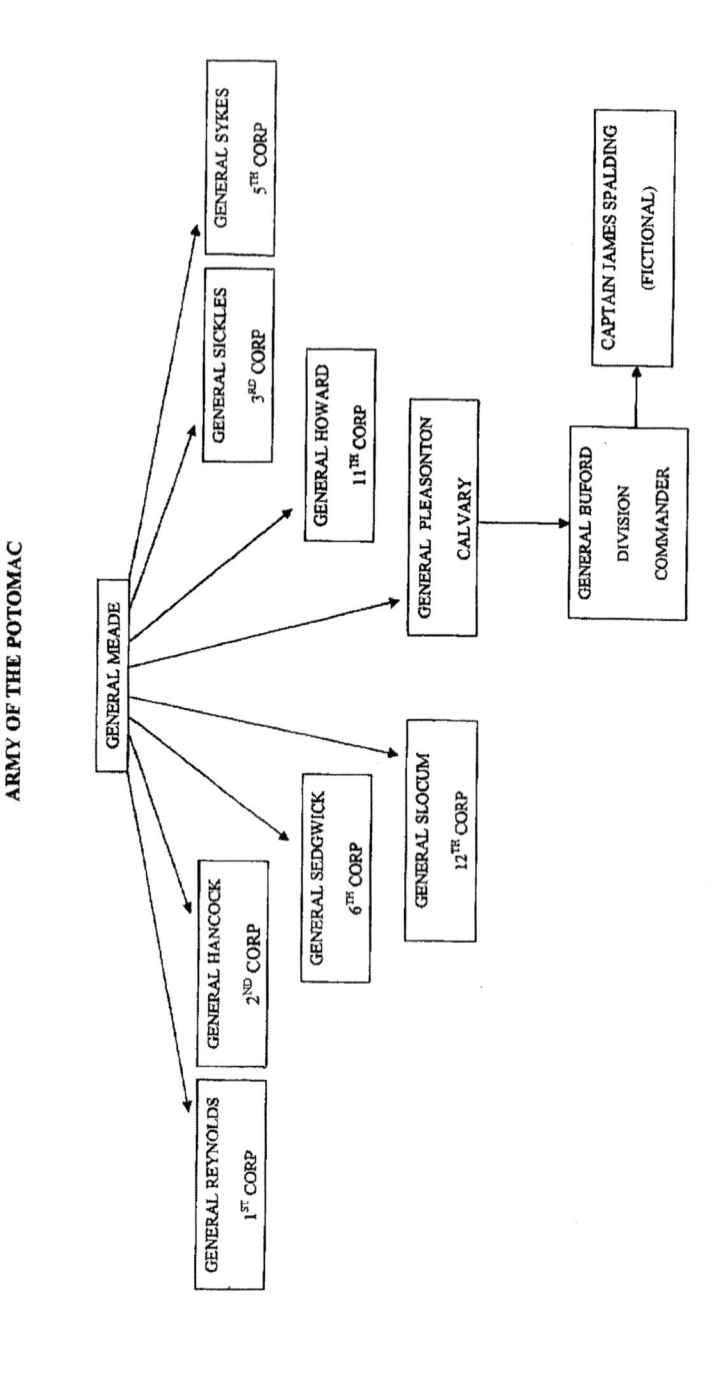

- GENERAL MEADE
  - GENERAL REYNOLDS — 1ST CORP
  - GENERAL HANCOCK — 2ND CORP
  - GENERAL SICKLES — 3RD CORP
  - GENERAL SYKES — 5TH CORP
  - GENERAL SEDGWICK — 6TH CORP
  - GENERAL HOWARD — 11TH CORP
  - GENERAL SLOCUM — 12TH CORP
  - GENERAL PLEASONTON — CALVARY
    - GENERAL BUFORD — DIVISION COMMANDER
      - CAPTAIN JAMES SPALDING (FICTIONAL)

CPSIA information can be obtained at www.ICGtesting.com
Printed in the USA
BVOW072207111012

302793BV00001B/48/P

9 781624 193774